Praise for *The Importance of a Piece of Paper:*

"In Jimmy Santiago Baca's haunting story collection, intricate family dramas . . . play out against the luminous, wide-open backdrop of New Mexico. . . . These debut stories are redolently, lyrically, evocative of their setting. . . . Throughout, Baca's prose remains as light-saturated and unsentimental as the rugged terrain—both geographical and human—that *The Importance of a Piece of Paper* charts with cartographical precision."
—Mark Rozzo, *Los Angeles Times*

"With his first venture into short fiction . . . Baca has enriched the genre and exposed another facet of his multidimensioned literary talent. . . . Baca renders the passion of the people and the beauty of the terrain in the same kind of vivid, robust language that characterizes his uncompromising poetry."
—Cecil Johnson, *The Philadelphia Inquirer*

"Inspirational, tragic, and redeeming . . . Baca provides moving poetic imagery and unleashes his gift for finely crafted sensory details."
—Lorenzo Chavez, *Rocky Mountain News*

"[Baca] speaks the truth through the people in his stories. . . . You can visualize him sitting with pen and pad in hand, sketching out a painful memory from his childhood. . . . The ideas are solid, especially when he . . . writes what he knows and stays true to himself and his experiences."
—Julie Ann Vera, *The Albuquerque Journal*

D1247662

"[Baca's] writing has a surreal touch, occasionally blurring boundaries between the seen and the unseen, a quality that feels consistent with his bloodlines. An insistent theme of redemption blends with an unexpected lyrical tenderness, confirming that even in the harsh landscape of his stories, Mr. Baca sees a horizon of hope. . . . Understanding can bridge a cultural divide, he implies, and he uses his well-chosen words to point the way."
—Tony Beckwith, *The Dallas Morning News*

"[Baca] continues to mine his experience, exploring conflicts between the rich traditions of Chicano culture and a modern world impatient with them. . . . His imagery. . . is always striking."
—Joan Keener, *Entertainment Weekly*

"Set in the writer's home state of New Mexico, many of the Mexican-American characters struggle with a yearning to be loyal to family and culture while at the same time coexisting in a mainstream society. . . . The stories transport the reader to a vividly drawn world where nature and animals come to life and marginal yet tender characters make their way in the world, searching for family."   —Sandra Marquez, *Hispanic Magazine*

"A collection of short stories that show the full dynamics and complexities of real life . . . Jimmy Santiago Baca's writing is about such struggles and about the degree to which loneliness makes people do things that hurt one another."
—Roger Soder, *Phi Delta Kappan*

The Importance of a Piece of Paper

JIMMY

SANTIAGO

BACA

The Importance of
a Piece of Paper

Grove Press
New York

Published simultaneously in Canada
Printed in the United States of America

FIRST GROVE PRESS PAPERBACK EDITION

Baca, Jimmy Santiago, 1952–
    The importance of a piece of paper / Jimmy Santiago Baca.
        p. cm.
    Contents: Matilda's garden—The three sons of Julia—The importance of a piece of
    paper—The Valentine's Day card—Enemies—Mother's ashes—Bull's blood—Runaway.
        ISBN 0-8021-4181-1 (pbk.)
        1. Hispanic Americans—Fiction.   1. Title
    PS3552.A254I49 2004
    813'.54—dc22   2003057089

Grove Press
an imprint of Grove/Atlantic, Inc.
841 Broadway
New York, NY 10003

05 06 07 08 09   10 9 8 7 6 5 4 3 2 1

Contents

Matilda's Garden
1

The Three Sons of Julia
17

The Importance of a Piece of Paper
45

The Valentine's Day Card
105

Enemies
113

Mother's Ashes
133

Bull's Blood
155

Runaway
181

The Importance of a Piece of Paper

Matilda's Garden

The day after they were married, Guadalupe drove Matilda in his old, flatbed farm truck, rattling down the long potholed and gullied dirt road, and parked in a field his family used for grazing livestock. He described the house he was going to build for her. It would be of adobe, with hardwood floors; the living room windows would face east with a view of the Sangre de Cristo Mountains; the kitchen would look out on the sheep sheds, hay barn, and tractor shed; the pantry and enclosed back porch would be divided by an archway separating them from the kitchen.

When they got out of the truck, he continued to gesture where the solid-core cedar back door would be, how it would open to the west and north fields, and how the three bedrooms would look out on the mesa to the south. The entire house would be heated by two wood stoves. To the east, he would dig a ditch from the *acequia madre,* or "mother ditch," which had water in it year-round, run it through the property, and build a small pond and bridges where the ditch meandered through the yard into the orchard and pastures.

As he talked, Matilda became thoughtful as she gazed over the grassy meadows. He was afraid she might be having reservations. She was wearing blue canvas slip-ons, a light green skirt with green nopal cactus patterns, and a white blouse trimmed with red thread. She walked around nimble as a pronghorn deer, turning one way, looking at him, her eyelids squinted, the morning sun reflecting off her raven hair, blazing it to an even darker black. She knelt to sift earth through her palms.

"Is there something bothering you?" he asked, perplexed by her sudden distance and worried she might not like his plans.

She didn't answer.

He watched her, awed by the familiar sensation that she seemed more an extension of nature's trees, grasses, and wild flowers than the offspring of humble parents. He recalled the first time he had seen her, how bored he had been in church that morning, gazing out the windows east to the Sangre de Cristo Mountains. She was singing in the choir for Easter morning services, wearing a knee-length white skirt and yellow ribbons tied to the tips of her long black braids. Light diffused from the stained glass window above the choir loft and bathed her in luminescence. When she sang, the doves fluttered on the window ledge and sunlight turned red and gold and blue as it passed through the glass panels, transforming Matilda into an angel in her descent from heaven, sent to earth to specially bless his heart that morning.

When he had kissed her the first time after their fourth date, he could taste the fragrance of sage and its indescribable spicy resin on her lips. And when she had caressed his face one evening lying down under an elm tree by the river, her fingers smelled like wild honeysuckle vines. When they went to hear his uncle play violin for the San Pablo fiestas at the church, he danced with her and she moved the way his uncle's violin bow careened across the strings, firm and elegant, provoking a desire in him to swing her all around.

Now he studied her walking quietly, biting her red and shapely upper lip: He followed her eyes like a crow staring intently at oval cherries on an uppermost branch. She blended in with the grass and the lush alfalfa's blue blossoms swaying heavily with the breeze coming in from the Rio Grande river nearby.

She finally turned. "This whole place will be a garden, and you I will nurture with the utmost love and care." She came up to him and kissed him. She reached down and picked up two small grains from an ant pile. She held one out to him pinched between her index finger and thumb. "Put this under your tongue, make a wish, and spit it out. The ants carry it to their place of dreams and it will come true."

"I already have my dream," he said, and looped his arm around her waist. He pointed to a huge roadrunner speeding past with a lizard in its beak. It leaped up on a fence post, tail twitching, head jerking in short jabs as it gulped the lizard down.

That was more than fifty years ago. He had been seventeen years old; she sixteen. Now the old adobe house creaked like an ancient, Mexican garden ornament, built more for flowers to inhabit than humans; the heady aroma of Matilda's gardens swaddled him in a blanket of heavy, humid sweetness. She was right, of course; she had made the whole farm her garden and nurtured him with her love.

Flowers and vines spread even into his dreams. Their scent had smoky shapes like blue herons and hummingbirds and parrots, drifting and transforming into cranes as they broke through the dream surface from the depths of his mind and into the reality of another dawn and woke him. He could swear, as his eyes adjusted to the dark in his bedroom, that he saw white wings fluttering midair across the room and he heard Matilda's voice coming from the field beyond the window.

He looked at the clock: 4:12 A.M. The chill had come early in late August, leaves tinged yellow, Canadian geese and sandhill cranes migrating south to the Bosque del Apache Wildlife Refuge. He turned over onto his left side, snuggled deeper under the quilt, tucked it under his chin, and pulled back the loose blanket to his left where Matilda used to sleep next to him. He stared at the stone in the place where her head would have been. It was now exactly three months since she had passed away.

He was crazy to believe she might appear because of the stone, and he knew it. Matilda had found it on one of her hikes to the mesa where she'd go for the seasonal herbs that grew there. The stone was sheared smoothly in half and fit comfortably in the palm of his hand. The cut side had a light blue horizon, a dark brown range of mountain ridges, and a white moon rising over them. For weeks now, after settling himself into bed, he had placed the stone next to him hoping his personal ritual might summon her from the spirit world to visit him briefly. Of course, he didn't believe it would, but he was certain that these private rites would somehow let her know that he was always thinking about her, and that consoled him.

Since her death he'd been clutching the stone for hours before sleep, rubbing it with his old, calloused thumb, whispering her name until he fell asleep. He believed he could retain some residue from her sweat or skin on his fingers. It started with the stone, but soon encompassed other of her possessions. Believing that she could feel his contact, he would take her favorite head scarf, hold it to his nose, and breathe in her smell. On one occasion he spent an entire day collecting the strands left in the bristles of the brush she used to comb her long gray hair. He would pray while he held the twisted braid of her hair along his wrinkled lips, sometimes even tasting it. He had finally twined it into a knot and placed it in a small leather pouch she had given him that he wore around his neck for good luck. He lay in bed a moment longer, thinking how strange his behavior had become, and yet it pleased him because it kept him believing he was in touch with Matilda.

A few weeks before, absorbed with memories of her and desiring a deeper, visual connection, he had decided to construct an altar with her favorite saints—Our Lady of Chestahova, the dark virgin; La Virgen de Guadalupe; San Martin de Porras; and some strange god from India that Matilda loved, Hanuman Ji. He collected everything he could find that belonged to her and set it on the altar. Every morning he rose, and with somber sincerity, sliced an apple and placed the cut pieces on a dish so that her spirit might have something to eat that day. And only after communicating with Matilda through this sacred rite would he begin his day.

The alarm clock on the bed stand rang and he pushed down the button. He got up and dressed.

In the last week or so he had been thinking about her last inhalation. In his dreams she was trying to breathe again. Her breath became wild purple lilacs in his mind, their vines curling out everywhere, so real to him he was certain that one day the driveway would brim with them. Wild purple lilacs swinging in the wind, seeds blooming at the front door, tendrils shaking against the window glass, nestled in the crevices, purple petals cascading off the roof. Maybe it was her spiritual self working through these images, creating a bridge from her world to his. All he knew was that somehow she was communicating with him in the way that she loved most, through flowers.

Without her, it had been difficult for him to respond to other people. Beyond accepting condolences from friends at the cemetery, he'd had no inclination to converse. He let his daughter or one of his sons handle the conversations with people interested in sharing experiences they'd had with Matilda. He found he was comfortable living in a world without them, but not without her. He was there in body but otherwise absent, and he trained his thoughts and feelings on her so intensely that some people attributed his lack of attention to the fact that he was losing his mind.

He went into the kitchen, flicked on the light, filled the teapot with water, placed a spoon and the jar of instant coffee on the table, and sat down. He opened last Sunday's newspaper and leafed through it while waiting for the water to boil.

He scratched his gray stubbly chin as he read the lead article, thinking he wasn't crazy at all, not compared to the rest of the world. Sixty miles east, in a town called Roswell, Martian-seeking tourists, drawn by rumors of alien spacecraft having landed there, were streaming in by the hundreds to view the extraterrestrials. The writer quoted some of the visitors as saying they had seen spaceships land in their fields or swearing they'd encountered aliens roaming ditches at midnight, suddenly coming up on them walking home alone. As he finished reading the article, he dismissed any lingering fear that he might have had about becoming senile—thinking of his Matilda's breath exuding from the plants was his way of coping with her absence, and he wasn't going to bother himself over what others suspected might be happening to him in his sudden isolation and silence. He was certain the breathing he heard in places around the farm was Matilda trying to speak her presence to him.

The day before she had passed away, while sweeping and cleaning the kitchen after breakfast, Matilda had reassured him that she was going to be all right. That Monday evening she took to bed complaining about having trouble breathing. Later, he sat with her in the bedroom and read the Bible, hoping to revive her spirits. They talked and she told him she was expecting to be up in time for morning coffee. After she had fallen asleep, he lingered at the window with his back to Matilda fast asleep in bed behind him.

Her wrenching gasp interrupted his thoughts and made him turn in fear. She panted forcefully, choking for breath. She sat upright, bulging eyes startled by a seemingly frightening specter hovering above the bed. Her chest rose, neck swelled, teeth clamped in a defiant fight to breathe. He looked around the room, wanting to challenge whatever sight had wrung the life from his sweet Matilda, desperate to strangle it with his age-mottled hands.

She fell back on the bed, staring up at the plaster ceiling as if some spirit had violently dragged out her breath through her opened mouth, her eyes open wide in frozen terror at its strength and size.

He had cradled her in his arms, repeating not to worry, he was there, his chin against her matted hair, hollow, gaunt shadows on her fevered face, purple rings around her eye sockets, his hands rubbing her clammy neck, her sweat-drenched nightgown clinging to her bony shoulders. She groaned for all the air in the room, in the house, in the universe. And then, after a time, she sighed her longest, softest exhalation, her breath blowing the curtains and seeming to turn the windmills patterned on them; the alfalfa outside sucked in her breath, the cultivated field soil, the wild green forest by the river, the tractor paths between the chili rows, the rutted road sloping upward toward town from the river bottom, all seemed to inhale her last breath.

"Oh well," he heard himself say, and sipped the last of his coffee. He pulled on a light faded cotton jacket over his denim overalls, patted his straw sombrero onto his balding gray-haired head, and before going out he wiped down the kitchen counters, hung the dishrag over the sink faucet, and turned off the light. He took her prize-winning rose from the bell jar inside the china cabinet and put it in his jacket pocket.

Outside, in the tractor shed, he pulled the choke and coaxed the gas pedal until, on the third crank, it sputtered and coughed into a low unsteady idle. He backed out slowly across the front yard, went alongside the sheep pens and around the barn, behind the house and along the orchards to the fields to the west. His headlights swept across the wall of cottonwood trees and, underneath them, the evergreen bushes Matilda had planted, and briefly lighted his handiwork—warped planks set on sawhorses lined with mason jars full of screws and washers, spools of baling wire, ancient tools, and rusting machinery parts.

The sheep bleated in the sheds. He drove past the mesquite corral where his three old nag horses whinnied and rubbed their sides on the stick fence. They'd all be fed already if Matilda were still with him.

He imagined her having coffee and toast, stripping a few ears of corn to check if they were ready for picking, tinkering with the tractor's carb, scraping off hardened dirt from the disc blades, snipping ripe tomatoes and chili peppers from the garden, slapping off dew from freshly picked garden vegetables against the sink sides. Matilda had his same wonder and love for farm life, and he couldn't express in words the immense satisfaction that welled up in him when he was in the field with her, shovels in their hands, soil under their sneakers, sweat pouring down their brows and backs.

His shepherd, Buster, came bounding out of the apple orchard to his right. He remembered how the dog had chased the truck to the chapel, dashing with tongue lolling the whole way. It was the farthest Buster had ever followed him, and while the priest gave his eulogy, Buster stood outside barking and scratching at the door. Everyone heard the dog but ignored him. Guadalupe was mortified, and in any other situation he would have given Buster a few good smacks, but he knew the dog was suffering some kind of trauma. Buster was up on the seat next to him now.

He turned the tractor onto a dry path between the rows and headed west of the house, to the open fields. He passed her vegetable garden.

The burly guttering of the tractor put him into a trance and he barely noticed Buster jump down. He let his mind ease into the exhaust stack's smoky incantation. It hypnotized him, droning in his bones and churning up more memories of Matilda when she had planted the windscreen of bamboo along the southern border of the fields. After that, she laced honeysuckle vines into the chicken wire, and it weaved over completely until you couldn't see the wire, leaving only a boundary bursting with aromatic flowers. The horses lounged next to it, tails swatting at the honeybees and ears perked alertly on the dazzling hummingbirds flitting in the blossoms. The headlights shone on water gushing through a break in a furrow at the end of the field. He reached back to feel for the shovel behind the seat.

The light crept up on the mountain crest to the east. Everything was waking up. It was Matilda's spirit in the plants. Sometimes before sunrise Matilda would sit in the semidarkness on the back porch steps and her eyes would glow with a brilliant sheen when she saw the mallards, red-tailed hawks, and crows gliding in at daybreak and congregating in the fields. It gave her a joy few other sights scarcely came close to—after meditating like that, she'd enter the kitchen, cheeks flushed and chilled, her eyes brighter than the morning sun, humming an old country song clear as a cathedral bell, ringing throughout the rooms with the immense pleasure of being alive.

He intended to patch the break, then close the sluice gate and irrigate the next field. There was still enough moonlight to see by so he turned off the tractor lights, put the gear in neutral, climbed down, took the shovel from the rope sling, and started rebuilding the dirt clods along the furrow, packing it solid.

From the channel brush came the sound of startled birds flapping frantically. It was Buster again, coming in from roaming the riverbank. He had crept up on mallards serenely floating in the ditch and barked as they scattered airborne. Sometimes he'd come back soaking wet and dirty with stickers and weeds in his coat, black nose scratched and bleeding from squirrels and wild cats, breathing hard, clutching an old muddy boot, a dead river rat, or bird in his mouth. In eleven years hardly a day had passed when Buster wasn't up on the seat beside Guadalupe as he ploughed and furrowed the fields. Clearing the dark treetops at the river, the geese wavered up toward the white moon. Seconds later, Buster came sprinting his way in a headlong rush from the Bosque.

Guadalupe heard him but didn't turn. Bent over, intently patting muddy shovel-scoops against the furrow side, he was caught off guard when Buster jumped on him, and he stumbled, losing his eyeglasses in the mucky water and dropping the shovel when he tried to regain his footing. He took a step forward, then back, and groped around for them in the water, his old, calloused hands turning up mud and pebbles but no glasses.

Meanwhile, Buster scrambled up on the tractor seat, wagging his tail and turning around excitedly. He barked at Guadalupe, lunging forward and bumping the gear stick, engaging it in low gear. The tractor moved, big back tires rotating slowly in the mud, catching little traction, sinking but catching now and then, and then inching forward. Guadalupe looked up and saw only a dark blur closing in on him. He tried to step out of its way, but he fell in the water and cut the bridge of his nose on the shovel blade. He toddled to his feet, lifted his right leg, and planted it momentarily on the slick muddy furrow side but slipped again.

The tractor tires churned slowly in the ooze, the motor humming hot, iron joints grunting, couplings grinding, bolts and washers straining as it inched forward in the mire, the droning groan of the engine laboring, the tires digging in deeper. The exertion of the vibrating tires loosened the furrow sidings, and water broke free, flooding around Guadalupe as he struggled to stand in the mud. The tractor suddenly caught hold of a rock and jumped forward. Guadalupe groped at the air hoping to grab some piece of the tractor and climb back on and turn it off. Then it leaped forward again and scooped him into its front-end bucket, which had tilted at an upward angle when Buster bumped the lever, lifting Guadalupe off his feet and carrying him now as if he were a branch. The tractor lurched then paused, moving until it went over the field boundary and crossed the road. Guadalupe struggled to escape—his body was half out of the bucket and he was ready to push himself off onto the ground when it butted him up against a tree.

There the tractor stayed, burying its tires in the soil, cleats chewing at the soft dirt, the sounds of loosening metal joints like a pig's snout snorting fiercely, biting and grunting at the earth with implacable hunger, slowly grinding deep wheel ruts into the dirt up to the axle, everything a blur to Guadalupe except his own imminent end. With the bucket's blade crushing his ribs, he knew he was going to die pinned against a tree, gazing straight ahead but unable to make out anything distinct except a gray light over the fields. He closed his eyes. Mixed in with the numbing of his body and his bewilderment was the fragrance of purple flowers, the smell of the manure and horses, and the panic that he still needed to talk to his children.

The idling tractor became inaudible. He felt heat flush over him, followed by a lightheaded euphoria. From the thick brush and trees of the Bosque, floating across the fields, came an old Mexican ballad, his favorite to dance to as a teenager with Matilda. He just had enough energy to open his eyelids to slits, but he could just make out the silhouette of a woman floating on the water. For a moment he thought it was La Virgen de Guadalupe, his namesake saint. She came across the fields and he desperately wished he had found his eyeglasses as she neared him. He was filled with the greatest delight, certain it was Matilda. Then he realized that he was her favorite flower, the one she had nurtured for over fifty years. He was the special flower in Matilda's garden, her cherished fragrant prairie bloom, which she came forward now to take and carry away in her hand.

The Three Sons of Julia

Julia set the bag down on her kitchen counter. She had bought garlic, lemons, avocados, Mexican sodas, red chili powder, red onions, lettuce, carrots, olives, and goat cheese. She had picked a variety of bruised and damaged fruits from the discount basket, apples pecked by birds, peaches and apricots that were blemished by weather and were small but sweeter and closer to what fruit tasted like when she was young. These were the fruits that had stayed on the boughs waiting patiently for a hand—the way her heart had waited, counting off the days every time she stepped out into the morning toward the bus stop for work and every time she returned from work, walking down the dirt road that had always seemed to her like a tunnel taking her further back in time. No sidewalks, no street lamps, dirt running right up to the foundation of the houses. Dogs ran wild, sniffing at scents from beans steaming in pressure cookers, red chili and sausage sizzling in frying pans, recently butchered pigs and goats' bones—she loved her barrio's ancient customs and even had a few primitive rituals of her own.

When her three sons were infants and one of them had a fever, she'd sit on the bed and lay him on his back between her legs. He'd play with strands of her long black hair cascading down her shoulders below her elbows. She'd rub him gently, massaging him affectionately like tortilla dough, working out the fever with her hands. Pulling and pressing, she'd soothe his body, tenderly mashing her face in his shoulder, nuzzling her strong brown hands under his arms, poking her fingers into his hollows, pushing at his hips, raking his back with her fingernails, rubbing his neck, pushing as if she were trying to move him uphill, away from the fever.

She now wished sometimes that she had someone to massage her pains away. She was prematurely graying, her complexion was harsh, wrinkles converged on her face from all sides, she was overweight, but most lamentable, she didn't have the optimism needed to enjoy life anymore. Washing laundry at the hospital all day for the last thirty-eight years had worn her out. But today she was full of energy, she didn't feel lonely as she usually did, wasn't thinking about her exhaustion or her body wanting to flop down on the bed and nap. All she cared about when she finally reached her two-room house and wearily stepped up on the porch clutching her groceries was that her sons were coming today.

She saw her oldest, Ramon, not as the successful investment banker he was now, but as the thirteen-year-old she held in her arms one summer evening during a dirt-lot football game. He had hurt his back and could not move. She'd gently rolled him over, lifted his legs again and again, dug her fingers into his shoulder blades, fingering the grooves along his spine with one hand while rubbing his neck with the other, until he became water sifting through her hands—free and loose and coursing again, out the door into the yard to resume his game.

Her middle son, Omar, now twenty-eight, had been touched by the angels and did not recognize the same reality as others. Instead, he spoke with the wind, was attached to plants and animals, drifting happily in other zones usually inhabited by spirits. He lived with her and spent his days murmuring at the breeze, mimicking frogs, chasing grasshoppers and lizards in the yard. Looking into his eyes, she saw his mind—a gold-winged butterfly fluttering in a permanent world of rainbows.

Darker in disposition was her youngest, Terrazo, twenty-six and passionately proud of being a rebel. When he was eighteen, he had slapped a drug dealer in the face and was shot by his bodyguard. He managed to drive home, where Julia cut the bullet out from his stomach, applied herbs, and knelt all night at her altar praying to La Virgen. She never told him that she believed her prayers carried him like a branch in a river raging toward death back to the shore of this life to her arms. Her promise to God that night for sparing his life was that she would sacrifice her own aspirations and dreams in devotion to her sons.

She kept that promise and it now seemed fulfilled by their love on this day, the Fourth of July, the first time in nine years they would all be under her roof again. She'd been marking off the days on the calendar—the ones preceding the Fourth were *x*'ed with a black marker, the Fourth was circled in blue. The three large candles she had bought a week before still burned on her altar; every morning she lit the incense and asked God for one day with all her sons, and now her prayers had been answered and the day had finally arrived.

She checked the pot of beans and red chili simmering on the stove and covered them. She went into her bedroom, coiled her long graying hair into a bun at the back of her head, rubbed herbal salve on her ankles and hands that ached from arthritis, took her special turquoise blouse and red skirt from a cardboard box beneath her bed, and dressed. Then she went back to the kitchen, stood by the window over the sink, and started making her salsa and green chili.

She watched through the window as she prepared the salsa, lingering on the house where Eloy used to live. He had started with one small restaurant years ago and now had them all over town. He bought a million-dollar home in the rich part of town and moved. Julia sometimes cleaned homes for extra money, but never a million-dollar house. It must have a lot of empty rooms and what good is one's dwelling if it is always empty. Life passed too quickly to spend your money on big empty houses. The boys had been infants not too long ago and she too was getting on; she felt it in her bones and muscles.

Beyond her small adobe home in the barrio, on a winding dirt road by the Rio Grande, was the hospital. She knew that on the twelve floors above the laundry where she worked, doctors and surgeons were trying to keep people alive. They could cure anything but lack of love, and not having love in their lives was, to her mind, what made people sick.

She could smell their loneliness every morning in the sheets, the doleful odors of sickness and death in the fibers. She could visualize the child who had broken his bones on a skateboard because his mother or father didn't come home until ten each evening and the house was too empty and lonely to be in. She could smell the faint perfume of a woman who had been in a car accident, out drinking because her boyfriend no longer loved her; and the man dying from liver problems, his grief permeating the sheets. They all came from empty houses, lonely places. She'd sometimes go upstairs during an emergency to deliver sheets to a certain ward and see patients in excruciating agony in their rooms; then, hours later when she'd be called in again to change the sheets, she'd find that the patient had died, but the room was still filled with their loneliness.

Yes, life was all too short, and gazing out the window, seeing her reflection in the glass—graying hair, tired brown eyes, chapped lips—she smiled thinking her children had taken the best of her, absorbed her in their pores. She had poured her life into them, urged out sad aches from their hearts, protected them in a violent world, and given them happiness.

Familiar barrio kids went past her view. They ignored the dogs, who barked and meanly cowered behind their fences because kids had pelted them with enough stones to teach them that if they ventured out, they were going to feel pain. She inhaled sage and garden fragrance and it momentarily dizzied her, much like copal and myrrh transported her during Mass. A stray cow wandered into the field of grass between her house and her neighbor's. With a smile she recalled how Ramon, now thirty-three but six at the time, had been outside with other kids peering at a steer through the slats of a livestock trailer.

One of them accidentally elbowed the trailer door latch and freed it. She saw it in her mind, running wildly down the road as people dashed after it the way they did in Spain during the chasing of the bulls. The best part was that a dog had locked its teeth into the steer's tail, and it veered this and that way trying to lose the dog, but the dog clung fast, flying through the air as though it had wings. It was the funniest scene.

Up the road, shirtless men and their girlfriends in tank tops flapped back the tarps to their red, white, and blue tents, opening for business with impressive fireworks displays. She didn't particularly like firecrackers, but nothing and no one was going to spoil her day. To her left, crows flew from the mist bordering the river a half mile away. The trees were submerged in fog except for the one huge branch she could still see, magically floating like a green feather suspended midair. In fields extending out from the riverbanks, buckskin and palomino horse heads appeared poised on mist, but as they grazed forward, tails and legs slowly revealed themselves.

Kids laughed as they threw firecrackers at Mr. Montez, who was watering his front lawn. He went to hose them down but they dashed away, climbing like goats over stacks of fruit and vegetable crates. They thought they had gotten away, but Julia watched as Mr. Montez quickened his pace, rounded the corner of his house, caught them in the open, and drenched them. He laughed as they scattered. The road started filling with others: shiny lowriders; daughters in nice clothes driving to their parents' for a visit; denim-clad, hard-hatted laborers rattling by in old trucks pieced together from junkyard parts; shy clerks in modest attire walking to bus stops; adolescent boys walking with their girlfriends giggling into their cell phones. The world was waking up, and her special day was finally starting.

The pressure cooker's whistling steam startled her. She turned from the window and there was Omar, standing near the stove in his pajamas and staring at it with wide eyes. After feeding him and helping him dress, she sent him outside to play on the wide stretch of grass beside the house, where he rolled from one end to the other, over and over.

Julia was stirring ground beef into the chili when Ramon, his wife Susan, and their daughter Lila walked in. She set the wooden spoon down and turned, wiping sweat and hair strands from her forehead.

"Mama, *cómo estás?*" He hugged her.

"You look so handsome," she said. He filled the kitchen like a beautiful giant and she admired him proudly.

He looked around at the pots simmering on the stove, food in clay bowls on the counter. "Mama, I swear, your beans and tortillas . . . smelling them, I go crazy."

"Well, then, Ramoncito, pitch in—you used to eat more tortillas than an army."

He hung his suit jacket on the chair back, unclipped his cuff links, rolled up his white sleeves, turned the tortillas on the hot plate, and stacked and covered them with a towel.

She and Susan embraced, then Julia knelt and peeked at Lila hiding behind her mother.

"You going to give me a little hug?"

"If I do, can I go outside and play with Omar? Please?"

"Of course," Julia said, "he would like that."

Lila gave her a quick little kiss and ran out.

Susan took a glance out the window to check on them, sat down, and fanned herself with a farmer's market flyer that had been lying on the table.

"They get along so well," Julia said and went back to stirring the ground beef.

"Ray, have you told your mother the good news?" Susan stood at the sink next to Ramon.

"What news?" Julia asked, giving Ramon a questioning look.

"We're moving," Susan said, "into the country club area. And we're going away for the summer. Europe. You know we met there when we were in college. Our bus broke down in a small town in Tuscany and we stayed in a monastery. Ray and his group were going to Rome and some mix-up in transportation forced them to settle in for the night at the same monastery."

"That's wonderful," Julia said, looking out on the lawn. She half listened to Susan, straining instead to hear Omar and Lila through the open window—her squeal of excitement as Omar, with arms extended like helicopter blades, whirled round and round, head tilted back, until he became dizzy and fell. She had come to distinguish his shrill giggles and strange sounds of fear, happiness, and confusion. He was happy.

Julia turned from the stove and placed steaming chili sauce on the table covered with a plastic nonslip coverlet. "Tortillas are done, beans cooked, salsa made—ah, I'm sorry, would you like coffee?" They declined but she poured herself a cup and sat down. "Well, we'll wait for Terrazo."

An hour or so later Terrazo pulled in. He was with a bunch of guys and Julia could tell he had already been drinking. She kept repeating, "Thank you Lord, thank you Lord for bringing my son back to me." She went outside to greet him and cried, touching his face as if to reassure herself he was really there, caressing his cheeks, holding his arms. She tried to stifle her joyous tears but couldn't.

"Mama, it's okay, I'm fine," Terrazo said.

"Come, come. Ramon's here, Omar will be so glad to see you. Let's eat."

Omar came rushing around the house. He clapped when he saw Terrazo, who took his brother and whirled him around until his feet were off the ground. Alarmed that Omar might get hurt, Julia ordered Terrazo to let him go.

Ramon, with Susan next to him, stood outside on the stoop holding the screen door open. "Welcome home, little brother, hope you're here to stay this time." He looked at his brother's bulging forearms tattooed with red winds and yellow fire, water rising with a ferocious blue face, and earth wielding a machete and beheading its enemies. Even his fingers were tattooed, each alternating a smiling and grim-lipped skull face. On the inner part of his arms sand blew into the eyes of a blood-dripping statue of lady justice holding the scales, one dish stacked with hearts and the other with gold coins piled high.

"Actually I'm going back this afternoon," he replied, his voice tinged with spite.

"What?" Julia gasped.

"He's kidding, Mama," Ramon said, but he wondered how long it would be before Terrazo started partying with all those girls again and ended up using heroin and failing his urine test at the parole officer's and eventually being sent back to prison.

"I'll make you all plates in a little bit," she told Terrazo's friends, and they thanked her as they took six-packs out of the car, admiring Ramon's new white Cadillac, and walked to the end of the driveway to the backyard. Susan watched them anxiously and then went inside.

Julia set out plates and served everyone. Lila and Omar sat on the floor in the living room, eating off a little coffee table.

Julia knew Susan merely endured their rare visits. She picked lightly at her plate, hardly eating. She acted nervous as if she felt out of place, constantly smoothing her dress, keeping her manicured hands on her lap, her posture erect. But she made Ramon happy and that's what counted, although Julia had yet to see them hug or kiss in public.

"What a pretty suit," Julia said.

"Tailored flannel. It's a little hot, I should have worn my T-shirt and shorts," Ramon said.

"On Sunday? Are you kidding me? Don't get chili on it, it'll never wash out," Susan said.

"Blue's my favorite color," Julia said.

"It's a summer suit. I don't know what he'd do without me," Susan said. "I want him to grow one of those Zorro mustaches, a pencil-thin one."

"Do you shave him too?" Terrazo asked.

"Make sure he gets regular checkups, at his age, for colon cancer. You know my brother had it, caught it in time, and is getting treatment for it," Julia said.

"I go to the doctor's every three months. Don't worry, Mama, I take good care of myself," Ramon said. "I mean she takes good care of me."

"You got the easy life," Terrazo said, as he rose to help himself to another serving. "If you want to get rid of that paunch and those flabby arms, I'll show you how."

Ramon rose, went to the stove, and heaped his plate with beans and rice. He towered over his brother by a foot, but Terrazo was taut as a bowstring, built like a boxer in training.

"If I didn't have anything else to do but sit in a cell all day, I might have time to work out too."

Terrazo's friends came in, respectfully greeted Julia, then lined up behind one another at the stove, piled their plates, and went out. The neighborhood kids Julia often fed stopped by to grab a burrito or taco and a cup of Kool-Aid and left. Friends drifted in briefly to say hi and share in Julia's happiness. All over the yard groups of kids played, teenage boys gathered with their girls, and by the bonfire, men and women, some with guitars and others with congas, drank and laughed. The dusk filled with firecrackers and howling dogs, kids laughing. Julia was happy. This was how it should be.

Back in the kitchen, Julia was covering the dishes of food with tinfoil. "I remember," she began, "you used to sit right over there, Ramoncito, doing your homework. And late at night you'd get hungry, and everything I had covered up and put away would be out all over the counters in the morning."

"It was that glass of warm milk and cookies you set on my desk every evening as I studied," Ramon smiled, "that gave me the brains to pass my tests."

"And how you used to worry me," she said to Terrazo. "I was always at the window, praying, looking out anxiously for you. And of course, the authorities would call as usual because you had missed school again."

"I never liked school. I remember you at the ironing board all night, ironing Ramon's clothes, mending his socks, making sure he was always dressed the best."

"Because *I* went to school," Ramon added.

Terrazo glanced up at him. "People learn a lot more by experiencing life, not reading about it."

Julia studied Terrazo for a moment. "You seem angry . . . I know, you just came out, and that's a terrible experience to go through, but—"

"Just happy to be home, Mama." He refilled his plate.

Ramon ate silently. Susan continued to pick at the little she had on her plate.

Julia asked, "Are you all right?"

"I'm dieting." Susan frowned.

Julia rose to serve more beans and rice to Lila.

"No, she's had enough," Susan said.

Julia smiled at Lila and wished she could have told the girl's mother, Let her be a child. Had she been able to speak her mind freely with Susan, she also would've asked why they didn't bring Lila over to visit her more. It seemed that whenever she called for Lila, Ramon said she was over at Susan's parents' house, with their big swimming pool, barbecues on the veranda, and more toys than the child could ever use.

"You got anything lined up?" Ramon asked. "It's going to be awful boring for Terrazo, hanging out around here all day."

Terrazo looked at his brother. "Jose asked me to help him get some of those cars out of his garage. Mama, you got any more lawn chairs?" She shrugged, and he said, "I'll be outside." He put his plate in the pan with warm soapy water in the sink.

As Terrazo was walking out, Ramon said, "We make a lot of loans to businesses and I can call in a favor if you want."

"Take care of yourself, Ramon, looks like you got a lot more on your plate to finish than I did."

"Don't go too far, we still have dessert," Julia said.

"Come on, Omar, let's light up some firecrackers." Omar jumped up and followed Terrazo.

Lila followed behind Omar. "Mommy, please . . ."

"It's cool, she can play with the other kids," Terrazo said. As long as Terrazo had known Lila, she always had to stay clean, sit on the chair or couch, and was never allowed to play with other kids and get dirty.

Susan had reservations. "Ray?" She was afraid of Terrazo's friends.

"Keep an eye on her and don't let her go running off with the other kids into other yards." He kissed Lila and she followed Terrazo outside.

"Are you sure?" Susan's blue eyes flashed with warning, a cautionary look that questioned Ramon's decision. "Ray?"

"Relax, she'll be fine." Ramon then asked his mother, "Mama, you're not going to baby him again are you? Don't let him loaf around here all day taking advantage of you. Last time he got out, he started living here and dealing drugs right out of his room."

"Let me enjoy my son for a while, he just got out. I need to see him here, be with him, be together, and you too, you don't come often enough."

"He's a man now, treat him like one, Mama." He paused. "I'm sorry, I'll drop the subject. And Mama, I promise I'll come over more—we've just been overwhelmed with business. We're in the middle of expanding our market into Dallas and Phoenix, and the bank is . . ." Ramon continued but Julia wasn't listening.

She turned on the sink tap and felt content. The water seemed to have a memory of her hands. She liked washing dishes, the comforting feel of warm liquid pouring off her knuckles, which vanished underneath as if the soapy bubbles and swirls were playing a game with her fingers, remembering her hands as fish, and they became fish again, whirling, swimming, lifting, and submerging in it. She lost herself in the memory of the faucet stream, transforming her hands back into brown fish, surrendering to its warmth and softness.

As she finished the dishes, she studied her hands again, now heavy, swollen, and wrinkled like elephant pads stomping through drought-baked days. These hands didn't belong to her, callused stone mason's hands, surfacing and plunging into the sink like carved rock animals, clacking among the cups and plates and forks and spoons. And as if some creature raised its head from the swamps to devour her in that instant, a scream came, and then seconds later Terrazo burst through the screen door, grabbed a bar of butter from the table, and was out again. He didn't say anything to Ramon or Susan but they were already out the door, right behind him.

Seconds later, Ramon saw Terrazo kneeling down by Lila and rubbing butter on her palm. The rest of the guys stared down, not saying anything, and other kids were gathered around Lila, trying to give Terrazo room but crowding in to see her hand. The kids were whispering frantically that it was an accident. One of them had lit a sparkler, and while it swung in circles through the air, Lila, seeing the sparks and the mirror glints, had grabbed at them, right where the sparkler was burning the hottest.

Looming over Terrazo, Ramon roared out with rage in every word, "What the fuck are you doing, you idiot! You never put butter on a burn!"

Susan grabbed Lila, crying, "Oh my God, oh my God, it's a third-degree burn, we have to get her to a hospital!"

Instantly, Ramon shoved Terrazo aside and swept Lila up in his arms and headed for the car. They took off, the wheels erupting a cloud of gravel and dust. Julia looked at the driveway after they left, then turned toward the group by the bonfire. The kids were playing again, chasing one another on the broad half-acre of grass on the side of the house. The men and women stood around drinking beer and smoking, resuming their conversations—everyone except Terrazo, who was sitting by the bonfire staring into the flames, scratching the embers with a stick, making sparks and red flakes float up around his head and shoulders.

Ramon returned that evening around eleven after taking his wife and daughter home. Susan had forgotten her purse and Julia had it ready. Lila was going to be okay, Ramon said, but butter didn't help. He sat down wearily, apologizing for getting angry and upsetting everything. It had been a great meal, he said, but the whole incident enraged him.

"Why do you let them carry on like that?"

Julia fixed him a cup of coffee and sat down. "You know it's a tradition, and Terrazo just got out, he deserves to have a little party. That's how it's done, it's better to have him here with me than in a bar, getting in trouble."

Just then Terrazo walked in. He went to the refrigerator, took out a twelve-pack of beer, and glared down at Ramon.

"If you have something to say—say it." Ramon usually dismissed people's contempt—he had seen it in the eyes of both brown and white men when he walked down a street with Susan—but tonight he felt like intimidating, not being intimidated.

"You ever talk to me like that again in front of my friends, I'll break your face in half."

Julia spooned and stirred sugar in her cup. "You're not fighting tonight." She looked toward the living room where Omar was watching an old black-and-white cowboy movie. Omar glanced at her, peanut butter on his chin. She blew him a kiss that he blew back, like a soap bubble through an *o* he formed with his fingers.

"Putting butter on her hand was the stupidest thing. When are you going to check in with the real world?"

"Respect each other," Julia said.

"Respect?" Terrazo said, setting the twelve-pack down. "*He's* the one who has to learn to respect people, punk ain't got no respect for nobody."

"Am I supposed to respect you," Ramon said, getting up, "because you have all those tattoos, you been in prison . . . ? I'm not afraid of you . . ."

"You better be; I'm not the little brother you can push around anymore. You with your gold watch, gold rings, money, fuck you . . . you don't impress me, you sold out, punk, sold out, turned your back on your own *raza* . . . how many Chicanos did you deny loans to today? Oh, I see, you only work for the rich people . . ."

"Was I supposed to be successful like you? A successful drug addict, a skilled thief, a child who refuses to grow up!"

Julia got between them. "*Por favor de dios!* Stop!"

But Terrazo couldn't and Julia saw that strange look on his face, that hard ground on metal blade look in his eyes that hadn't been there before he went to prison. He had changed. Something in him had broken down, gathered itself around a seed of anger rooted deep in his blood, and grown into rage, awakening and breathing in him.

Terrazo moved past Julia in a second and grabbed Ramon and hurled him back. Instantly he was on his brother, squeezing his neck, blocking Ramon's punches with his elbows. Terrazo growled, "Don't ever talk down to me. You haven't earned that right. Every time you do it, you'll pay for it."

Ramon used his wide hips and huge legs to throw Terrazo off. They rushed each other and rolled along the cabinet made by Julia's cousin Louey, a carpenter. The special dishes and glasses and the picture frames with photographs of her and the kids crashed to the floor. Then they tumbled into the counter, thudding hard against the wood, fists pounding at each other's bodies. Blood sprayed from Terrazo's mouth. A welt swelled around Ramon's right eye.

In the living room, crouched behind the La-Z-Boy recliner, Omar was shivering, shaking his head back and forth, slapping himself across the chest and arms, mumbling to himself. Julia knelt on the floor and rocked him in her embrace, soothing him with cooing sounds, covering his ears and eyes with her hands.

Meanwhile, Ramon hurled Terrazo against the sink, where he cut his hand on a cup shard. They locked into each other, gritting teeth, sweating, cursing, freeing a hand to hit the other.

"Think being in prison makes you a man, you bastard! It's for losers, you got it? You're a fucking loser!"

Terrazo spat back, "You think coming down here with your *gringa* wife, showing off your money, makes you better? Kissing that white ass makes you a lackey sonofabitch!"

"Get over it—the world doesn't owe you shit. I love her. So she's white, so she's a *gringa,* fuck you and all your friends howling about pride and race and power. Pride to destroy yourself! Power to kill each other! Enough is enough little brother! All you ever do is moan and groan and complain about what the gringo has done—robbed your land, taken your culture—it's all bullshit. An excuse for you being a failure. A fucking two-bit dope fiend!"

They lunged, knocking over the kitchen table, upending the chairs, grappling on the faded, linoleum floor where as children they had propped a broom under a blanket and pretended they were camping in the woods—the floor where they slept together, their arms and legs entwined into a single braid of skin and bones, needing each other to survive in the world.

Julia's tears fell into Omar's black hair that smelled of grass and leaves. Her eyes were far away as she took Omar's fingers and kissed them, whispered to him how lovely the night was, how they were going to have ice cream and cherry pie later.

Ramon had grabbed a heavy stainless steel soupspoon and smacked Terrazo across his cheek, cutting it. Terrazo kicked him in the ribs and cracked two as Ramon shrieked with pain. Ramon's torn white shirt was streaked with blood, his face bruised, his eyes purple and swollen. Terrazo's face was oozing red from the mouth, his cheek cut and neck scratched and clawed. The toaster crashed to the floor, then the enamel coffeepot. They fell back, punching recklessly, grabbing and slugging each other and holding on tight, then slugging again.

Julia stared at the food all over the floor and, nearby, the shattered picture frames that once hung on the wall above the TV. There was one picture of her and her husband Frank when they were married. Another one of Frank and all three of the kids on the yellow backhoe he used to drive. Then another one on Sunset Boulevard in Los Angeles, the summer they went to Disneyland, taken in front of a crazy shop that sold scary masks from famous movies; another one in front of the Chinese theater across the street.

But the photograph her eyes lingered on the longest was a large frame with seven smaller photos inserted in a circle pattern. These were the photographs taken when her boys were between the ages of ten and fifteen, when they were the closest—one photograph showed them roaming the Rio Grande riverbank all day, another earning a few dollars working in the apple orchard, and another captured them swimming in the ditch—in every picture they were smiling and laughing.

She went to the stove, picked up the big silver pot with the red chili in it, and threw it at them. Scalded, they had no choice but to stop. She set a chair upright and whispered for them to sit, and they picked up two chairs and sat across from each other. They glared at each other.

"This day was my day, the only thing I asked of you was to let me have one day . . . one day . . . but you couldn't, could you, no, no, your needs always come first."

They could see she was trying to control her anger but it was rising in her strained voice, in the sharp edge of her words.

"Mama," Ramon started but she cut him off.

"Which mama are you talking to?" She looked at him with tears streaming down her face, then screamed, "Which mama?"

Ramon was speechless, confused.

"The one you're ashamed of, that your family thinks is stupid and backwards? The one you never visit because you're too damned busy. Tonight, you betrayed me."

Julia turned to Terrazo, "And you, which mama am I tonight?"

Terrazo said solemnly, "I'm sorry, Mama, I'm sorry."

"No sorries—no more," Julia said. She heard firecrackers and gunshots and she heard herself say, "It's the way things are. Your friends, drinking, smoking weed, laughing. You cared more about being with them than with me." She looked at both of them. "Why? Why? Why couldn't you let me have even a day that was mine? It was too much to ask, too much."

She rose, paced around the debris on the kitchen floor, and started picking stuff up. When they tried to help, she lifted her hand and said, "I'll do it."

She glanced at Omar and saw him peering frightfully from the blanket she had wrapped around him on the floor. She smiled. She picked up the photo of the three of them and stared into the smiling brown faces of her children. Omar was in diapers, Terrazo in cowboy clothes, hat, and holster, Ramon in a suit. She wiped the blood off the photo, nodded to the boys to help her, and they picked up the table and set it on its feet. She took the chairs and arranged them. She placed the photo on the table and sat down.

She retrieved her purse from the floor. She opened it, took out a leather pouch, plucked two plastic packets of hair from it, and put them on the table. "When you were born, I cut locks of your hair and carried them for good luck, all these years." She took two more plastic packets from her purse. "These are your umbilical cords."

She took out a bunch of dollar bills and looked at Ramon. "Is this what you live for?" She tore the money into small pieces and threw them at him.

Ramon said, "Mama, what are you doing?"

She screamed, "Which mama are you referring to!" She stood in the middle of them. "The mama who worked day and night for you without ever even a thank you?"

She turned to Terrazo. "Or the mother who took you food every weekend in jail?

"The mother who worked extra jobs, cleaning houses and taking wash in and sewing clothes, to get you through college, Ramon?"

Then back to Terrazo: "Or the mama who went on a date, and when she came home, you wouldn't let her touch or kiss you good night, because you accused her of whoring around?

"Ramon, do you remember, I went dancing one night? I smelled of a man's cologne, you told me I had beer on my breath; you said that I was a bad woman because I didn't stay here like a saint every night of every day of my life? One night I go dancing, and you accuse me of being a whore!"

She looked at Terrazo. "Do you know how hard it was to go every Sunday, every Sunday on a Greyhound bus two hundred miles round-trip to get one hour of visiting with you?" Terrazo started to say something but she cried, "Say nothing!" Her eyes were dark and furious. "How many times, my little Terrazo, I sat here worrying for you. How many times did you ever help? Not once. You were too much of a man, too tough to help your mother mop the floor, clean the bathroom. Pick up your clothes. You threw everything on the floor, the couch, the bed, knowing your slave would pick it up. While you were out drinking, taking drugs, proving you were a man, getting more tattoos, going back to jail, I worked to send you money so you could have your candy bars and cigarettes.

"And you, Ramon, old enough to cook but never once did you cook a meal for yourself. You waited until I came in from work to do it. Yes, I was a slave and a whore. And look at me now . . ." She was feeling light-headed.

"It's the Fourth of July." She paused, looking around at the mess, and said quietly, "Leave me alone. Go to your wife and daughter. Whisper to each other about how it is unsafe here, how this is not a good place to visit. Go Ramon. And Terrazo, you go with your friends, fight, prove you are a man, do your drugs—leave me and Omar."

They got up, both bending down to pick up broken plates, but she cried, "Leave!"

She went into her bedroom, put on her nightgown, brushed her hair, lotioned her face and arms, and came back out. She sat on the couch and after a while heard them leave. With the base of her palms pressed against her eyes, she wept for a long time.

She wiped her face and walked into the kitchen. She slowly climbed up on the counter and opened a cabinet above the stove and reached way back. She never drank and this was old stuff she'd saved for years for a special occasion. The label read "Chinaco Tequila." She uncorked it, poured herself an amount equal to four shots, and then walked over to Omar.

"*Salud mejito,*" she toasted and drained all of it but a small swallow for Omar. "Here," she said, and Omar took it and drank it, grimacing from the hot taste. She knelt beside him and asked in a soft voice, "Omar, do you want to dance? Come . . . let's dance." Omar's eyes were darting at every firecracker sound, and to calm him, she said, "Hear the dogs howling and barking? They don't like the noise either."

She helped him up. He stood there, arms hanging down, hands picking at his pants. She went to the closet in the living room, took out the old phonograph, and set it down. She turned on the porch light, and then carried a kitchen chair out to the tiny porch facing the dirt street. She carried the phonograph outside, set it on the chair, plugged it in. She took Omar by the hand and led him outside.

She put on an old Mexican record, placing the needle on her favorite song, "La Paloma Blanca." It started scratchy and she turned it up. She positioned him in front of her and he followed as she led and talked to him. "This is the song your father loved so much." A few minutes later Omar's attention was drawn to a leaf blowing across the lawn and he raced after it. Julia turned up the volume as loud as it would go and music sailed into the neighbors' windows. She danced alone as neighbors came to their doors in pajamas and stood in silence watching her.

She swung her invisible partner around, dreaming she was again in the arms of her husband who had left years ago for Mexico and never returned. Sometimes, she thought, the heart's memories are more real than anything else. She was with the very first boy she had ever dated, Lorenzo, and he swung her, gliding her through the steps, her head tilted back, her hair falling over her shoulders and down her back. She turned, dizzied by her own fantasy, and laughed as firecracker rockets shot up, spraying red, blue, green, and gold colors across the night sky.

Her legs no longer hurt, her knees no longer burned with arthritis, her gray hair turned black and lustrous, her waist shrunk to a size twenty-six, and the wrinkles and worry grooves on her face smoothed to a sixteen-year-old's unblemished glow. The fireworks ceased, and the night sky filled with her Mexican music. Sparks from the dying bonfire crackled. The neighbors stood mesmerized by Julia. She did not see them or hear Omar whimper when he rolled over on his hand and twisted his pinkie, nor was she aware of dogs slavering at the chain-link fence by the road. She was her boyfriend's sweetheart again, and she danced under the porch light and didn't even feel her bare feet crunch on the broken beer bottle glass, leaving her bloody prints on the concrete slab with every happy dance step she took.

The Importance of a Piece of Paper

Adan arrived in Albuquerque very late at night. After visiting briefly with his sister Marisol and brother Pancho, the youngest of the three, he was so tired that he went to bed. A few days earlier he had called to say he had some important business to discuss with them.

Marisol rose at five, content that they were together, and went outside to collect eggs, having decided to make their favorite breakfast. She rummaged around the sheep pens, in the chicken coop, under bushes where the Rhode Island hens liked to lay eggs, and when the wicker basket was full, she set it down and pitch-forked armfuls of hay to the sheep and horses. Then she sat down on an old willow chair under an apple tree and watched the morning sun slowly crest the Manzano peaks to the east and wondered what was on Adan's mind.

She walked over to the small bridge and leaned on the railing, looking into the water at her reflection. She knew she was still pretty even though she hadn't had a boy tell her as much since her college days. Her beauty was in her distinctive contrasts; her eyes and hair were dark as crow feathers, and her almond-brown complexion was like the smooth sand in the ditch that ran by the junipers. Her voice was vibrant as a green leaf, drifting out around her as though twirling in the ditch water's uninhibited clear current, easily riding its meandering course.

She heard a flock of Canadian geese somewhere overhead. In the arroyo sage tree to her left, a red-tailed hawk swooped down and perched, bouncing buoyantly on the limber uppermost branch, watching the fields for a mouse. The cries of the migrating geese got louder, and then as the dawn light grew, she saw the formations of geese and mallards flying high in the sky. The light was on in the bedroom where Adan was working on legal briefs on his laptop. Pancho had gone into the barn to feed and groom his special horse, Zapata.

They had their lives set, they were doing what they wanted, and Marisol occasionally felt a painful jolt of regret that, at twenty-eight, she still hadn't completed her masters. A year ago she had quit her studies in the Chicano department at the university in Albuquerque when her mother died from an illness, followed by the death of her father in a gruesome car accident. She had planned on returning to her studies after her father's funeral, but then life took her in its momentum and carried her to this point.

At first she had only planned to stay a while and help her brother Pancho care for the farm. The farm didn't yield much money, and with the hundred acres they had inherited and the little money their parents' insurance had left, they barely made it month to month. They sold alfalfa, apples from the orchard, sheep from the flock, and they leased out pastures to ranchers for grazing their cattle.

Pancho applied his energy and attention to training Zapata and spent days away from the farm, traveling hundreds of miles with friends to look at horses rumored to be good racers. Marisol also stayed on the farm because she worried Pancho's temper would land him in serious trouble. Over time, she hoped to teach him to handle his affairs with people in a more easygoing, diplomatic manner.

Before their parents' deaths, he'd been married and living in a trailer with his wife and baby girl in Belen. He got it into his head that his wife, Isabel, was having an affair while he was off training horses. He went to a bar one night and beat a man nearly to death, and after it happened two more times, Isabel was so afraid of him that she left. He never got over her leaving him, even though it was proven later that she had been true to him. Now, every two or three months, he'd take off for a few days, get into some drunken brawls, and come home and be fine for another two or three months. Marisol couldn't leave him alone to run the farm.

Pancho still couldn't even talk about his little girl. At the mere mention of her name, he'd spiral into a brooding mood for days. And Marisol couldn't talk to him about what interested her—the books she had read, documentaries she'd seen on PBS, lectures from controversial writers she'd downloaded on her computer. She still held the hope that one day she'd be able to return to finish her master's degree.

She got up and walked back to the house. Entering through the back porch door, she placed the basket of eggs on the counter near the window, and with her right hand on the slop sink, leaned down and slipped off her dirty boots and grimy socks. She ran cold water over the soles and with a wire brush scraped off clumps of mud and manure. She threw her socks onto a pile of dirty laundry in the corner next to the washing machine. Her black hair was pulled back in a ponytail; she had on jeans and a red and blue plaid shirt with its tail tied in a knot at her waist. Her features were blushed red from early exertion in the cold fields. She placed her boots inside the door against the wall to dry and then went into the kitchen and turned on one of the stove burners.

She took the coffee can from the cabinet above the kitchen sink, scooped out some coffee grains, and poured them into the coffeepot. She paused to watch Pancho cantering the black colt around in a circle on a training rope in the front yard. Pancho wore faded jeans, a rope belt and silver buckle he'd won bull riding in a local rodeo, the loose end of the belt hanging over his right leg, plaid cowboy shirt, scuffed tan cowboy boots, and a cowboy hat stained with grimy sweat lines. He was cooing to the colt, and soon its ears perked, its legs anxious to run. She admired the way he handled it, how colt and man worked in unison, the two of them becoming a single elegant creature. When Pancho looked at her, she motioned him in. Then she went to Adan's room and told him breakfast was ready.

After they had finished breakfast—fresh tortillas with red and green chili, eggs, and ham—all three relaxed at the kitchen table sipping coffee. Adan now set his leather briefcase on the table. Pancho straddled his chair from behind, resting his arms on the top of the chair back as his brother pulled out a manila folder and laid out the papers.

"Here's Mama and Papa's will," he said, looking every inch the successful lawyer in his blue suit, beige tie, expensive tan loafers, gold watch, and matching tie clip. "I've gone over it and want to talk about selling my part of the land."

The statement seemed to deafen Marisol and Pancho temporarily. It was as though he was speaking in a foreign language.

Marisol slapped flecks of hay off her jeans, bit on her upper lip, walked to the stove, poured herself another cup of coffee, and then sat down again. Her large brown eyes turned to Adan. "What?" A heavy silence hung in the air like an anvil on the verge of crashing down on them. "That's the craziest damn thing I ever heard out of you," she said. She looked at Pancho in wide-eyed disbelief. "Can you believe this?"

"It's bullshit," Pancho began. "You never really worked this farm. It's not in your blood. Since you were young, you've always been studying the books and still do. That's your life, not this farm. So how is it you figure you're entitled to sell land you've never given a shit about much less broke sweat over?" Pancho reached down and scraped dried manure off around his boot soles. He took his cowboy hat off, ran his finger back through his long black hair, scratched his scalp, and put his hat back on.

Adan sighed and clasped his hands on the tabletop. "Don't start bringing up our whole lives here Pancho. It's not a personal thing, not against you or anyone, I'm just selling what's mine in the will, what I inherited from our parents."

"Well, you can't do that," Pancho said, dangling a small length of rope over the chair and swinging it in small circles by his boots. He snapped the lasso up into his hand in one quick motion. "I need to get them horses fed and be with them the rest of the day. But before you leave, I want you to think about how this farm has been in our family more than three hundred years." Pancho was restless; he was by nature edgy with himself and others, more comfortable by himself or with his horses most of the time.

Adan said, "I understand that, but it doesn't change the fact that I need the money to get my practice off the ground." He knew it would be difficult for them to accept his decision because it had always been understood that the land was never to be sold or broken up. But he was determined to follow through. It was a matter of survival.

"We all need money to get something done, but not at the expense of our parents' wishes. I looked up to you for going out on your own, making it, becoming a lawyer. I used to talk you up to everyone. But lawyering has made you weak—you got no heart. You waited until Papa and Mama died to turn on them."

The silence between them swelled with a tension that was almost volatile. Each stood his ground, detached, until Adan, a red thread of anger in his tone, calmly said, "You want me to justify my decision to you, little brother. We haven't been close in the last few years. Sorry that my law school took all my time, that my visits became more and more infrequent and we grew apart. But don't ever say I stopped loving you or my family. Life took me in one direction, you in another."

The horses were neighing outside.

"Well, it's taking me out of this fucking bullshit talk." Pancho slammed the screen door on his way out.

"That worked out great," Adan said to himself in disgust.

The wind blew sharply against the tin roof. It banged against the corrugated metal sheds, making the sheep bleat nervously. Apple leaves scattered along the porch and flew across the kitchen window.

That evening when Pancho came in, Marisol got him to sit down long enough for her to lay out the plans.

"He's agreed to give us a chance to raise the money—he'll sell his share cheap to us. It doesn't have to leave the family."

"How the hell you expect to get the money?" Pancho asked.

"We could try a loan against the land we have. Maybe borrow it from someone."

"What the hell are you talking about!" He slapped the will papers off the table. "I'm not going over no will or anything else, we're not selling a pebble off this farm. And the last thing we want to do is give it to a fucking bank. It's against everything we stand for. Mom and Dad, their parents, and back generations all said—never sell the land!"

"It stays in the family," Marisol said. "He needs twenty thousand. The going rate is five to seven thousand an acre and we're buying his share at a thousand an acre." She paused, adding apologetically, "If he didn't need the money, he'd give it to us, but he needs the money . . ."

Pancho went to the window and stared out at the fields. He took out three leather strands from his back pocket and started braiding them in silence. He sighed, stretching his neck as if it were stiff. "How much time did he give us to get the money?"

"He didn't say, only that he needed it soon and that he couldn't hold it for long."

"I got work to get done . . ." Pancho said.

He went out to the barn, ran some water from the cold well-water pump, filled a tin bucket, and carried it into the stalls. He petted the horses in the corral and lingered by Zapata. The black stallion had his own covered stall. Chico, their blue heeler, dashed in, leaped on him all soaking wet, and unconsciously Pancho sprang at him with a clenched fist, ready to beat him. Chico barked and whined back into a corner, then ran off through the barn door.

He was beside himself with anger. He unlatched Zapata's stall gate, snatched one of the leather reins hanging on a post nail, and haltered the horse. He led him out into the evening, rounded the corner of the barn, and decided to ride him bareback in the Bosque, along the Rio Grande. He mounted him, heeling the horse hard in the belly, and galloped across the field, water splashing at the horse's hooves up to his knees.

★ ★ ★

Three weeks later, Pancho raced Zapata against the county's best horses. County races were occasions for farm and ranch people, prairie people, foothill and mountain folk from the area to get together and share news and have a good time. The well-to-do horse owners parked their new trucks and expensive shiny trailers together. They wore mothball-smelling Stetsons, aviator glasses, squeaky new alligator cowboy boots, starched creased Wrangler jeans, stiff white-pearl-button Western shirts, bolo ties, and leather vests.

The getting-by folk came with rusty trailers hitched behind their dilapidated pickups and parked them around the field. Their kids rode old mares, chased after goats, and lassoed sheep. Under cottonwood trees, teenagers brushed down their ponies, flirted with girls from other towns, and dreamed of one day competing in the national rodeo finals. Small-time ranchers scouted around to buy bulls to mix in with their herds or to exchange a cord of firewood or hay for a colt that might turn out to be a good racer. Others set beer coolers under card tables, stoked hot coals to smoke burgers on portable grills, and drank Jack Daniel's in lawn chairs under trailer awnings with their country wives.

They watched as a grader leveled a track around the field. No amenities, no bleachers, no hot-dog stands or toilets. Racehorses arrived and cowboys gathered to check each one out, taking note of what kind of trailer towed it in, how it got off the trailer ramp, how the trainer treated it, whether its nature was easy or high-strung, how the rider rode it, whether it shied from other horses or challenged them with defiance. Pancho and Marisol drove in and parked their shabby horse trailer alongside the old pickups.

Most riders and trainers had heard about Zapata, and there was growing excitement to see him race. You could feel the observers' mounting expectation flow into amazement as Pancho backed Zapata out and led him around on a halter. And when Pancho ran him back and forth to limber him up, heads nodded, impressed with the new blood on the scene, now believing the rumors that had spread through the whole lower Rio Grande valley—that the black quarter horse was something to see.

Many of them knew that Pancho had bred three generations of champion mares, and had worked on two of the best equestrian farms in New Mexico. While the owners bet on their own horses, many of the riders secretly laid their money on Zapata. It was Labor Day weekend and there were more riders and horses than usual, and a lot more money coming out of billfolds.

Zapata won four elimination heats and placed first in the final race, proving beyond everyone's expectations that he was the champion to contend with now. People could scarcely believe how fast he was at two years old, beating out the favored big bay thoroughbred by five and a half lengths.

Marisol and Pancho were both elated: They had made the money needed to buy Adan's twenty acres. After the races, Marisol wandered around with girlfriends, visiting other camps until they found one where musicians were strumming guitars and violins and singing *corridos*. Pancho gathered around a bonfire with the rougher crowd and drank with his old buddies. Their camaraderie was noisy, and they joked good-naturedly until, as always, Pancho had one too many shots of mescal or one too many lines of cocaine and challenged the biggest of the cowboys from another village to a fight. In the morning someone told Marisol where to find her brother and she went looking for him in a woman's trailer. It was good timing, because the trailer was already hitched to the truck and they were ready to pull away when Marisol stopped them and found Pancho inside, fast asleep in the woman's arms.

Despite his hangover and a few bruises, Pancho was in good spirits as they came down the dirt road leading to their house by the river. Marisol was counting money stuffed in a brown envelope. They had gambled all they had to buy out Adan's part of the land, and they had won.

"He wasn't even trying and he beat them," Marisol raved proudly. She sealed the envelope and threw it to Pancho. He caught it and kissed it. "He could have trotted the last quarter mile and still won," Pancho boasted. "I'm going to enter him in the Albuquerque and Santa Fe races. There's a big entrance fee, but he'll win. We're talking serious bucks. For starters, I'm buying you new clothes, a nice pickup. A new tractor—a dually— fix the house up a little, build some pipe corrals, training rings, and—" Pancho stopped midsentence as they cleared the hill. He stared at the new BMW parked inside the open gate off to the side.

A tanned man in his late thirties with sandy hair, wearing a blue blazer, casual slacks, a white shirt, and brown loafers, was looking over the fields.

"Who's that?" Pancho asked.

"I don't know." Marisol's excitement soured.

Ranchers didn't trust a person with an easy smile. Life was too hard to smile that easy, and if life had been such that a person could go around smiling openly at strangers, the rancher's homespun opinion was that the man lacked character or was trying to hustle you out of something he hadn't earned.

Pancho pulled up beside him. "What's your business?" he asked, a guarded caution in his voice.

The stranger stepped closer to them. "I didn't quite hear you," he said, and maneuvered around cow droppings, not letting his pants catch on any briars or tumbleweeds. The sunlight brought out auburn highlights in his hair; even his eyebrows had dusky red bristle mixed in with the light brown. His eyes were blue, glowing as clear and translucent as a piece of ice in light. Marisol noticed the scar on his chin, the small indentation on his right ear, the balding spot on the back of his head, his white teeth, the half-moon shadows under his eyes. She couldn't take her eyes off him.

Normally, she would have been the one to question a stranger, while Pancho remained sullenly quiet with an indifferent hostility to his attitude, meanness being an aspect of his character. He glared at the man, impatient with Marisol to ask him what his interest was here.

The stranger slipped off his calfskin gloves, reached into the breast pocket of his blazer, and took out some papers. As he did so he looked at Marisol with a kindness she felt ripple through her.

She fumbled for the door handle, got out, and latched the gate behind them. She looked down at the ground, feeling an overwhelming essence from the prairie rise up to her. It was inexplicable and unexpected to sense so strongly the prairie flowers and grasses, dizzying her as she walked toward the stranger standing by the driver's side of the pickup. When she was within arm's reach of him, she finally looked up and her eyes fixed on his longer than she would have liked.

"Hi, I'm Jaylen Maguire . . . your new neighbor. You must be Marigold? And Pancho? That's an awful nice-looking horse." He went to pet Zapata's head sticking out of the side trailer window.

"Keep your hands off him," Pancho growled, looking ahead through the windshield. "What do you mean *neighbor?*"

"I'm the new owner of this property."

"You're mistaken about that."

"I've got the deed right here—bill of sale too."

Everything seemed to come in from all sides of her experience and sift through the lovely sound of his voice, which seemed to pour purely into her, redefining in a unique and exhilarating way everything her eyes were seeing, her breathing, her standing there. And in this strange frame of mind—though maybe because she was stunned by the sudden news—she handed the

envelope to Jaylen and said, "Here's the money . . . for the land."
She noticed he wasn't wearing a wedding band.

He looked at her oddly. "I'm not selling it, I bought it."

"Get in the truck, Marisol," Pancho demanded. He glanced
at the man with enmity. "Don't forget to close that gate behind
you. You open it—you close it." He spun his tires, sending up a
cloud of dust and gravel in Jaylen's face. Pancho turned to Marisol.
"What the hell's the matter with you—what, are you mute and
deaf now?!"

She too wondered about her peculiar behavior and didn't
say anything until they parked in front of the house and went in.
Marisol threw the envelope on the table in the living room and
picked up the phone. Pancho got on the extension. When Adan
answered, she cried, "You get our land back! We have the money
to buy your share."

"I already sold it. I didn't think for a second you'd be able
to come up with the money. How did you get it?"

Pancho yelled, "Zapata won the race—"

Adan broke in, "I didn't know about the race."

"You can't decide on your own—just sell the fucking land—
we're all in this—can't do that." Pancho threw the phone down
and yelled at Marisol, "Hang up on his ass, we'll get our land
back our way!" Pancho stormed out of the house, slamming the
door.

She stood at the kitchen window listening to Adan apolo-
gize for not waiting a little longer, regretful that he didn't know
about the races. As he talked, she watched Pancho. He was

under the tractor shed with a big toolbox beside him, and in a fury he started dismantling the hydraulic lifts on the front end of the tractor. Beyond him, dark storm clouds gathered on the horizon. She felt disoriented, fearful. She told Adan she would call him back and hung up.

After a while, Marisol took out some boxes from her parents' closet and started sorting their belongings. She could hear the rain outside. It started as a light patter at first and grew into a thunderous drumbeat. Her mind floated back to Jaylen; she felt a deep contradiction in the lingering way he looked at her as if he were some familiar instinct, older than their combined years.

With each load of clothes that she washed and ironed and folded and then placed into cartons and stacked on the porch for Goodwill, Jaylen's features surfaced in her mind. They didn't fade until she finished the clothes and started sifting through her parents' personal things, which they had kept in shoe-sized cedar boxes with bear and wolf designs on the lids. She had never looked in them. Now she was amazed by the contents.

The boxes contained each of the children's umbilical cords, wrapped in sandwich bags. White infant booties each of them wore after birth. Belt buckles. Blue beaded sandhill crane tail feathers. Bolo ties. Silver bracelets. Turquoise rings. Old coins. Necklaces. A red woolen bag filled with arrowheads, a leather pouch filled with rocks shaped like moons, trees, mountain ranges, and other rocks imprinted with fossils. Marriage photos. Eyeglasses. Jeweled pendants and hair clips. Black-and-white snapshots of Adan, Marisol, and Pancho at various stages of growing up. Newspaper clippings of poems and prayers. Old pocket-knives and ancient pocket watches. Matilda's silk headscarves. Guadalupe's Mexican leather billfolds.

She heard the screen door slap shut and expected to hear Pancho in the bathroom, but he entered her parents' room where she was kneeling on the floor, surrounded by the scattered items from the keepsake boxes.

"We gotta get that asshole out of the mud."

She looked up at him, wet, wiping his hands on a rag. Grease and smoke smears smudged his face and clothes.

"What?"

"That gringo up the road—he's stuck in caliche. That brand-new car of his don't work as well as it does in the city." He frowned, muttering at the inconvenience, "Sonofabitch!"

Marisol glanced out the window. "Looks like a gully washer . . ."

"Some of the road'll be washed out," he said. "I got the tractor tore down. We'll have to do it with horses before it floods that road away and his car with it. All we need is to get his car floating in our fields . . ." He grinned at his own joke.

The downpour was so heavy she could barely see out the back pantry window into the orchard. They pulled on their galoshes, gray raincoats, and cowboy hats. When they got to the gate, Marisol saw that Jaylen's car was stuck in the middle of the road. Just beyond the gate, the blurry image of Jaylen came running in the mud toward them, soaked to the bone in his suit clothes, coughing and shivering, his head to one side shielding it from the hits of rain.

Marisol drew up her Appaloosa, holding the reins of a big bay mare. The wind whipped the rain sideways and she snugged her hat on tight. Pancho dismounted Zapata. He got into Jaylen's new BMW sports coupe, shifted into reverse, and accelerated. Mud spattered everywhere from the rear tires. Pancho gunned it again, trying to rock it back and forth, burying the back tires to the frame. The rain was hard and stinging. Pancho got out, took the reins of the extra horse, and threw them at Jaylen. "Get on her."

Pancho tied three ropes to Jaylen's rear bumper, then noosed the loose ends to the saddle horns on the horses. Jaylen mounted his horse with some trepidation. Pancho knew by looking at him that he'd never been on one before. "Sonofabitch," he cursed, and spat. He swatted Zapata's rump and swung around fiercely, facing them. Drenched, he yelled, "We're pulling it to the side of the field, enough to get a truck through. If we need to, when the rain slows we'll bring up the tractor when I get it running."

Marisol nodded, rain pouring from her hat brim. Pancho motioned Jaylen to guide the horse as he was doing, easing it back step by step until the rope was taut. He and Marisol were on the ends, Jaylen in the middle. The horses strained back, foot by foot, their legs deep in the mud. They were slowly pulling the BMW out of the mire when Jaylen almost fell. He yanked the reins as he was trying to regain his balance and inadvertently forced his horse to whirl left. Instead of grabbing the saddle horn, he lunged one way and pulled back on the reins, causing the horse to rear wildly and spin again.

The rope somehow looped around his waist. Now spooked, the horse was hard to control and it stamped violently in a circle, swinging and shaking its ochre-colored mane and head, twisting the rope around Jaylen and drawing it tighter. Jaylen's face turned red. He had the breath knocked out of him, his eyes bulging as the big bay mare shook him back and forth like a lifeless mannequin on her saddle.

It was not something Pancho or Marisol expected. The extra, loose length of rope had tangled up around Jaylen's torso, and as Pancho maneuvered in beside Jaylen and reached out to free the tied end from the saddle horn, Marisol already had her pocket knife out and was about to cut the rope. With a voice louder than the thunder, he yelled, "Don't you ever cut any rope of mine for this sonofabitch!"

The reins slipped from Jaylen's hands, and Marisol held him up, her horse butting his as she grabbed the reins with one hand and with the other slipped the rope off the saddle horn. Jaylen lunged back, groping at the air, and tumbled down into the mud, groaning in pain from his rope-burned flesh. It took them a good half hour to finally get the car out.

Back at the house an hour later, while at the table having supper, Pancho cleared his throat and asked, "You feel like airing it out?"

"Airing what? That you enjoyed seeing him almost get seriously hurt?" Marisol said.

"Listen here, he ain't no one to me, and yeah, it would have been kind of funny seeing him yowling like a hurt pussycat. Something's bothering you," Pancho muttered. "What's going on?"

"What's going on, Pancho, is you better get over this bitterness you have toward people. I'm sick of it."

"You leave my bitterness to me, and tell me what's really going on."

"I don't want to talk about it right now," she stated flatly, forking her fried potatoes and pinto beans and corn together in a pile and scooping them into her mouth.

"Give me a little leeway on this, sis, I need to know," Pancho insisted.

"All right," she said. She put down her fork and gazed beyond his shoulder through the window above the sink to the eastern fields and treetops. "I think we should leave him in peace and let him have those twenty Adan sold him and be done with it. Put the whole affair behind us, we still got over eighty acres and that's plenty to work."

It was the last statement Pancho ever thought she'd make and it completely unsettled him. A hail of cold–hot energy soared through his veins and immobilized him for a few moments. "You have a thing for him, don't you . . . that's what's been bothering me . . . you and him."

She looked up at Pancho. "If I do?" The words came out wrong. She'd learned over many disputes with Pancho never to confront him in this manner. "Pancho, it's done, there's nothing we can do about it."

"Ain't nothing done," he growled. He got up without finishing his food and went to the door. "I'm staying in the barn from now on. There ain't nothing to say between us, least not till you come to your damn senses."

That evening Marisol kept the lights burning in the kitchen hoping he would come in. It was midnight and still raining. She showered and sat on the couch in the parlor. She could hear the crows cawing in the cottonwood trees, a blowing rain drafting arid scents of slaked soil and aromatic prairie sage through the house crannies. She went into her bedroom and put on her long nightshirt, imprinted with wild horses running across the prairie. She returned with a woolen blanket that she laid on the couch. She knelt by the fireplace and set a cedar log on the grate, lit some kindling, and got a fire going. She stood with the blanket wrapped around her, watching until it caught, and then she sat back on the couch. She inhaled and held her breath, and after a few moments, let it out with pleasure, releasing the day's exhaustion and stress. She combed her hair before the fireplace and then snapped a green scabbard from the aloe plant and peeled its smooth, taut skin with her fingernails, rubbing the peeled side on the scratches and small cuts on her arms and legs. After a while she threw the aloe frond into the fire and unscrewed the cap from an old bottle of Vick's mentholated ointment and massaged it over the length of her legs, deep into her sore muscles. She sat quietly for a spell, allowing the salve to permeate her aching limbs. Before she dozed off, she decided she was going to meet Jaylen on better terms.

The next morning, Marisol was startled awake by Pancho, who was riding the tractor close to the parlor window. He went around twice and then headed off to the fields. She sensed it would be a long time before he set foot in the house.

She dressed, made herself a cup of coffee, and sat at the table. She caught herself glancing repeatedly around the kitchen as if she were trying to remember something she had to do, and when she brought her cup up to sip from it, her hand trembled slightly. She went into the parlor and looked through the window at Jaylen's place. She saw he had parked an old trailer on his property for temporary living quarters. His car was parked beside a stack of new lumber and another pile of adobe bricks. She needed to get busy doing something and moved with impatient expectation, going from one room to another and back into the same rooms she had just entered. She felt a surge of adrenaline and decided to go for a walk in the Bosque to release it. She wrapped a shawl around her shoulders and set out for the riverbank, feeling a happiness she hadn't felt in years.

About a half hour into her walk she spotted Jaylen a quarter mile out heading her way on the ditch bank. They neared each other but didn't wave or give a greeting until they were a few yards apart. Jaylen began, "I was going south along the riverbank and I met up with your brother. I was exploring upriver, trying to keep within eyesight of a partridge I had frightened from a bush, when I suddenly came upon him."

She didn't respond. She looked off into the trees bordering the ditch.

"I didn't fully introduce myself. I'm Jaylen Maguire, an archeologist at the university."

That's how it started, and it grew from that day with them strolling the riverside and talking for a few hours. They walked and sat in some places and walked again, and Marisol thought to herself, with Jaylen's voice in the background, that this was how two people began a romance—natural as the breeze blowing her black hair across her face, the sunlight dappling the leaves and glowing in the spaces between arroyo sage and cedars, and a beaver carrying a branch, paddling along the inside edge of the ditch. She looked at the fading colors in the fields beyond her and saw the snowcapped ridge of the Manzano Mountains to the east, and like all things in nature, she felt the intimate hints of change coming over her thanks to Jaylen.

Over the next few weeks they walked and held hands, discovering new paths that wound and wove endlessly through the Bosque. Gradually they found thickets where they could kiss. They saw each other as frequently as they could. He worked three days a week, and the other four he was with her walking the riverbank.

They'd rest on fallen tree trunks, talking about his past and hers. Sometimes they jogged, other times she rested in one place watching the river and he went off running by himself and returned to her an hour later. With the passing days the leaves changed from faded green to yellow-brown and grayish gold and softly floated on the air around them, settling on the path they'd worn down on their walks. One Saturday morning they packed lunches and climbed the mesa to the west. It was an all-day hike. He picked wildflowers and she taught him their names. Coyotes stared at them, migrating birds flew overhead, deer perked up their ears at their passing in the distance, and toward late afternoon they walked alongside one of the irrigation canals and spotted carp and catfish in the muddy water. They nestled on the bank in tall river grass and watched big black-and-white Canadian geese glean seeds from grass growing on sandbars in the middle of the river. She taught him how to say the Spanish words *amor, confianza, niño, pescado,* and sometimes they were completely still, holding each other, mesmerized by the river, whose tiny wavelets enfolded seamlessly into one another in a dance of oneness.

On warm evenings, lying faceup on a huge fallen tree trunk in the Bosque, they gazed into the sky until the big moon rose over the Manzanos and floated up to the sky. One morning they drove to Albuquerque and lunched near the university. They went swimming in the gymnasium's heated pool. Jaylen took her shopping and bought her a turquoise bracelet with their names etched on the inside. Later they went to a movie about a couple falling in love and afterwards ate at a sushi bar.

This was how their lives entwined through the month of October, and Marisol never imagined the autumn days could be as sweet as they were with him.

One afternoon Pancho saw his sister walking on the riverbank with Jaylen. Anger twisted in his chest like a knife. He used his field glasses to spy on them and saw Marisol laughing hard at something Jaylen said. Pancho saw his sister's lips moving, and he would have given anything to hear what she said. She turned and did not look back as she hastily cut through the brush and climbed over fallen tree branches away from the winding path in the Bosque. She scrambled up the ditch embankment to where she could see Pancho's truck parked nearby in a field.

On one level everything seemed impossible—Adan selling his part of the land, his sister dating this gringo. Pancho's only solace was knowing that if Marisol wanted to be with Jaylen, she would have to leave with him and live somewhere else, and he knew she would not do that.

In the fall moonlight, he saw her watching him through the kitchen window as he and Red Wind, a sixteen-year-old Navajo boy, worked with the horses. Red Wind rode Zapata and Pancho trotted him around in a circle on a lead rope, training Zapata to stop, back up, go forward, turn sideways, and resume his gait. He fell into a trance while he watched Zapata go round and round, and summoned the face of his father. Guadalupe had never said much, but Pancho knew he wouldn't approve of Marisol dating a gringo. The two cultures seldom mixed. Whether anyone admitted or talked about it openly, the ill feelings between Hispanics and gringos were real and present. The differences went deeper than mere cultural customs; there was long-standing, deep resentment toward Anglos for what they had done to Chicanos in the past.

Pancho remembered hearing something about Jaylen being an archeologist and he wanted to tell him he wasn't impressed. In Pancho's opinion, he was nothing more than a grave robber digging up old relics and selling them to museums. And his brother Adan was no better, because he had no understanding of family loyalty.

Pancho spent the next week in the barn arranging harnesses, bridles, reins, ropes, saddles, and blankets in the tack room. He oiled his mom and dad's old saddles, stitched the edges where the leather fringe had worn thin, replaced bronze rivets with new silver ones. He limbered his new ropes, standing twenty feet back lassoing a bale of hay, roping and pulling the slack tight as motes of fine dust exploded in the air in the sunshine that slanted through the window and door. He replaced stall sideboards the horses had chewed on, and each rusty nail he yanked out screeched like the pain he carried inside himself. He salvaged the boards he could, sawing the chewed grooves straight and sanding the brittle splinters smooth. He nailed the one-by-six planks back, spacing them six inches apart. While he worked the smell of alfalfa and manure comforted something in him. He gathered kindling in the Bosque, chopped wood, and stacked it by the side of the house. The woodpile was perfectly even on all four sides, hardly an inch of any log sticking out from the rest.

The more he worked with Zapata, the more the ache in his heart slowly worked its way out of him. He rode bareback, lightly slapping the reins against his rump. Zapata bolted up the dirt road bordering the fields north of the house. Pancho turned him around, heeled his flanks, and felt that familiar calm ripple through his body as Zapata galloped, the muscled, brute velocity between his thighs thrusting him forth below the trees, the wind in his face, and his frustration scattering behind him like autumn leaves.

In the Bosque he chainsawed a clearing beside the riverbank where he and Zapata could lounge. One afternoon he was sitting on the ground, eyeing the glimmering river as it coursed south, when he saw Marisol and Jaylen walk by in the distance. A razor-sharp stone lodged under his skin pierced him. He knew this gringo didn't appreciate what he had. His purchase had no significance for him beyond owning a nice house in the country. But to Pancho, it meant past generations of relatives sacrificing whatever was necessary to guarantee the farm stayed in the family. From the youngest children to the grandparents, they shared the unspoken conviction that selling any part of the farm would bring dishonor to the family.

When he was a boy, he remembered his mother and father going off at daybreak to work as cotton pickers in order to pay the land taxes. They all worked extra jobs to pitch in and pay the taxes. What they grew they ate or used to maintain the livestock and seed the land for the following year. There was never a year when the farm made enough money to support the whole family, and everyone had to hire out to other ranchers to make ends meet. Each family member was as much a part of the land as their breath was to their survival. It was a spiritual connection, and that's why he couldn't understand Adan selling his part.

He mounted Zapata and walked him around the clearing, bordered by sparsely spaced Russian olive trees, sand cedars, and sage. He prodded his right heel into Zapata's side making him turn right, applied left-knee pressure to turn the horse left. After enough of this patient discipline he smacked Zapata's flanks and they abruptly climbed an arroyo slope. Pancho clamped his legs around the horse's belly, clenched his mane, and leaned low on his neck as Zapata broke into a headlong charge, rounding trees and dodging branches. He gracefully took the tree-lined curves, leaped over fallen limbs and roots bulging up in the path, lengthening his stride down a straightaway stretch.

On one occasion he found himself five miles south of the farm when he slowed, loping east along the irrigation ditch, then swinging north a while and west again to come in from the dirt road that led to the house. He had looped around to check out the twenty acres by the gate that now belonged to the gringo. He finally reined in, rearing to a dusty stop. He wasn't expecting to see Jaylen, so he dismounted and checked everything over. There were the surveyor's stakes and small yellow and red flags marking the twenty-acre boundaries. He walked around examining the grass, sifting dirt through his hand, and squinting his eyes as he scanned the fields and checked the irrigation ditch, all with the deep penetration of someone wanting the images before him to be eternally imprinted in his memory.

As the days drew on, Pancho noticed the increasing activity at Jaylen's place. Crews of Mexican laborers arrived in pickups to dig out the foundation footing for the house. Two backhoe men came out and trenched the septic hole; trucks from the Belen lumberyard dropped off pallets of supplies and covered them with blue plastic tarps. More day-laborers showed up to dig ditches, plumbers roughed in copper water lines and plumbing pipes, masons stacked cinder blocks and adobe bricks at various spots around the house corners.

He saw Jaylen come and go every few days, always wearing a suit, tie, and black dress shoes, and carrying a backpack with a laptop computer and books. He'd arrive early in the afternoon and wouldn't come out of the trailer until an hour or two later, dressed in jeans and a long-sleeved plaid shirt. He'd usually eat his lunch sitting on the bricks, and then he'd walk to the river with a pair of binoculars dangling from his neck.

One day Pancho took three ponies he was training for a rancher in Belen and went to the river. Jaylen was walking on a path in the Bosque, heading back to his trailer, when Pancho came around a corner riding Zapata so fast he almost ran Jaylen down. Jaylen stumbled to the ground trying to get out of the way and Pancho towered above him on Zapata, the horse stamping and snorting dangerously close to him. Pancho warned him to be careful about roaming the Bosque—deer came down to feed on the grass, and he didn't want to shoot Jaylen by accident. Though he frequently saw Marisol and Jaylen walking together, he never caught them in an intimate way. But he had his suspicions. And sooner or later, when he did catch them, it'd be hell to pay for both.

In the meantime, he occupied himself around the farm. He repaired the roof gutters on the barn, set the woodstove over the concrete slab he poured, and built a wall to keep the heat in the small room he was now sleeping in. He was up early changing plugs and checking oil and hydraulic fluid on the tractor. He attached the plow to the rear and pressed the lever that was supposed to lift it, but it didn't work, so he took off the crusty hydraulic hoses and replaced them with new ones. One week Pancho fixed the fence line along the west side of the fields; the next week he set in posts for new pens for the pigs and goats and the black Angus bull he'd won off a wager. He had big plans to start his own herd. He and some friends had gone down to the auction house in Albuquerque and had jammed a stock trailer with yearling calves they planned to breed to the Angus bull.

He drove his tractor to the post office in town and was happy to find in his mailbox his application from the state racing commission. On the way there and back he had to pass Jaylen's place, and seeing it made him think about his father and the way things were before. The last time they were together they had gone down to Onate's Feedstore, and after getting grain for the horses and cows, they had gone to Annabel's next door—a restaurant run by three sisters—and had breakfast. With their coffee, eggs, bacon, and hash browns with red chili powder sprinkled over all of it, they sat and chatted with the girls. They were the friendliest of people, all smoking and talking simultaneously: A woman sitting on a counter stool next to Pancho told him of her toothache; another woman sitting next to his father had had her fill of her man drinking and was leaving him. There were photographs of champion horses on the walls, horse calendars and trophies on a small shelf, and all of the counter stools were occupied by farmers in denim overalls with grimy feed-store baseball caps or by callous-handed, growl-timbered ranchers smelling of alfalfa and manure, vexed by the latest political bill that was taxing farmers out of existence. And because it had been so unseasonably dry over the last few years, with the rains coming so late when they did come, there were always some farmers who had just filed for bankruptcy or were preparing to. They would tell Pancho how lucky he was, that unlike stunted corn or baked fields with shriveled wheat that had driven them out of business, his colts would always be wanted, as Zapata was sure to be one of the champions with his photo on the wall.

The hot days that were bad for them were good for Pancho. With the leaves now fading into reds and yellows and the Bosque looking more beautiful than ever, Pancho took advantage of the weather. He and Red Wind took the horses swimming in the Rio Grande. To challenge Zapata, they rode him hard, bareback all the way to the other side of the river. The rest of the horses followed. On the other side of the bank, with the horses freely grazing in the brush, they sat and ate burritos on the bank.

"I used to pray here. Not anymore though, gave up on it," Pancho said, looking across the broad shimmering surface of the water. He wasn't expecting a response because Red Wind seldom gave one. It was his nature to listen, and Pancho liked that; often they'd go days without a word between them.

But he did reply this time: "He bothers you."

Pancho knew he meant the gringo and he didn't want to talk about it. He stuffed the rest of the burrito in his mouth. Red Wind smiled at him because green chili was dripping all over Pancho's shirt. Pancho picked him up, they grappled a second, then Pancho lifted him and tossed him into the river. They took off their boots and jeans and swam for a while, pointing out a falcon on a branch, a blue heron in the sandbar grass.

They rode back at a lazy pace, side by side. Pancho said, "They been kind of dating, walking and talking each afternoon. What do you think about that?" He looked up and pointed an index finger like a pistol at a line of snow geese. He squeezed the trigger. He kicked Zapata in the flanks and they roared across the high water, laughing and splashing, letting loose all their frustration.

A few nights later, Pancho sat on a vegetable crate in the barn oiling his leather chaps when the lights flickered. He glanced out the door and saw them flicker again in the house. He wondered if it was the storm clouds blowing in or his sister messing around with the fuse box in the pantry on the back porch. Sometimes she'd plug in the iron, the microwave, the coffeepot, and other things all at once and a fuse would blow. Anything, he guessed, to fill her time when she wasn't with Jaylen.

He didn't mean to be cruel to her by sleeping in the barn. To his mind, she just didn't understand how much it hurt him that she would go with a gringo. She was certainly old enough to remember what happened to their uncle Tranquelino. He clearly did. He must have been around ten years old when his uncle had gone down to the newly opened farm assistance office. It was a time when drought threatened everyone's livelihood—cattle, sheep, and horses were all near starvation and without assistance would die. Because his uncle couldn't read English, the government clerk refused to give him an application, and shortly after that, with the first serious snowfall, the entire flock had starved and frozen to death in the foothills. Only the gringos, who spoke English, got the assistance money to buy grain and hay. At his uncle's funeral a few weeks later, he couldn't help thinking that the loss of his sheep had something to do with him dying. Didn't she remember that incident and so many others over the last twenty years, and if so, how could she overlook those events and still like someone who had the same malicious blood and cold heart as the ones who stole so much of their land?

He turned from the barn door and took a vanilla cherry soda pop from the cooler, drained the bottle, and flung it into a fifty-gallon oil barrel to his right. He looked at the black clouds gathered on the horizon. It was going to be heavy, he thought. The pipe gate on the dirt road at the far end of the property glimmered in the lightning's intermittent glare. It was closed. In the flashes, he saw his neighbors' cows huddled in sheds and in the fields under trees—a few dull-brained cows, too stupid to know better, grazed on the shoulder of the dirt road that ran from the house through the fields up to the main village road. He should've graded it with the tractor blade, banked it away to the edges so water would drain to the sides. He took a couple of harnesses from the pegs on the tack room wall and started waxing them. The thunder and smell of coming rain made him feel content, and on nights like this he didn't mind being alone.

Zapata watched him from the stall, chortling with pride because earlier Pancho had brushed and combed him and he seemed almost conscious of how he shimmered like black obsidian. "You getting too big of a dang head," Pancho told him. "Lots of people heard about your running. Have to give odds now . . . you willing to put up our savings?" The horse whinnied excitedly as if he understood. "I'll put up what we have, you know that . . . we're going for broke, ole buddy . . ."

He was going to enter Zapata in the big state fair race and it was going to cost every penny he had. The purse was a half million dollars. There was no way Zapata could lose. Pancho was already planning in his head to add more stalls, more white pipe fence rails for training, buy more land, hire help. Pancho put the rags and wax cans away and petted and brushed Zapata one last time, then scooped a little of his favorite grain into a pail and watched him chomp it up with powerful jaws. He pulled the dangling lightbulb chain, shut the doors, and for the first time in weeks, went into the house to eat a warm meal and take a nice bath. Maybe it was time to make up with his sister. When he passed her bedroom, he stuck his head in and said, "Good night . . . and I love you, Sis, you got a crazy brother, thanks for understanding and hanging tough with me . . . sweet dreams."

Late that night, they were asleep and didn't hear Zapata neighing frantically, rearing to fight off the lightning flashes and thunder. They didn't hear the boards of his stall splinter when he kicked them apart and they didn't see him rush blindly out of the barn, crazed with fear and wildly galloping from the rumbling that kept following him. He couldn't outrun it but he kept trying, racing across the field, onto the road and out the gate that had been left open and was now whipped back and forth by the wind, clattering and scaring Zapata even more.

Earlier in the evening, Jaylen had come in late from filling out research grants at the university. He had opened the gate, but since it was raining so hard he thought better of getting back out of the car to close it. He was in a hurry to get out of the rain and minutes after he parked and ran in to his trailer, Zapata flew through the gate, the rain beating against his black shimmering coat like stinging bees.

Zapata galloped onto Main Street at the very moment Jose Velarde was barreling through in his Mack truck packed tightly with livestock. He was going to sleep at home tonight, then leave at dawn for the Amarillo stockyards. He was listening to a Mexican radio station and singing along with it, hurrying to get home to his wife, to a late supper and a warm bed. The windshield wipers were on high but rain still blurred the windows. Just then, while Jaylen was snuggling into bed under the feather blanket, and Pancho was in his bedroom asleep, a pencil and paper with which he'd been figuring up winnings and a horseman's magazine open on his chest, and Marisol was in her bed dreaming, Jose felt his truck hit something like a deer or stray cow. When the windshield wipers swung left and briefly cleared the window, he saw the head of an animal on his hood. It was a grotesque sight. Despite the blood still splattering his windshield, he could clearly make out a horse's head. He gasped with horror, made the sign of the cross, and screeched over to the shoulder of the road.

Pancho had a fitful sleep, tossing and turning, images of Zapata racing in his mind around a dirt track over in Sandoval, a small town forty miles northeast. He showered, shaved, and pulled out a clean pair of underwear, socks, an ironed shirt, and a pair of jeans from the bureau drawer. After dressing he set the coffeepot on the gas stove and then woke up Marisol. She came out in her housecoat and they sat at the table sipping coffee and eating buttered toast. He asked her about going with him to the race in Sandoval.

She clasped his hand on the table and smiled. "Give me a minute to wash up and get ready and I'll fix us something." They had two cups of coffee, a glass of orange juice, and scrambled eggs, fried potatoes, and green chili rolled in a tortilla.

When he went into the yard he found the blanket he had draped over Zapata and wondered how it got there. From a distance, he saw the splintered stall door and immediately rushed to the barn. The other horses were there but not Zapata. He tracked the fresh hoofprints to the gate and beyond, where a group of men in a truck met him. They were old friends. They stopped and got out before he reached them and stood watching him. Without a word, his friend Alejandro led him to the bed of the pickup and pointed to the blood-soaked sheet. Pancho flung it off and saw Zapata's head. His mouth struggled to form words but none came.

He couldn't move. Suddenly he looked around at the fields and trees and everything became explicitly clear to him. His breath quickened. The light became intense, the colors more vibrant, the air heavier in his lungs. He wanted to erase that moment. Something in him seized up and darkened his heart and he felt incapable of thought or feeling—he was numb—as if molten lead coursed through his veins.

He wasn't aware of walking back to the gate. He saw himself as though hovering above himself, outside of himself; he saw himself studying how the rain had not erased the tire ruts from Jaylen's car, how its wheels had spun ruts in the soil all the way to his trailer. There were small puddles of rain in Zapata's hoofprints. The sun glimmered in them. He felt the urge to kneel on the muddy ground and drink from the pools, hoping crazily that maybe Zapata would appear when he rose and turned and looked at the fields. He saw the smooth, dress-shoe prints that could only be from Jaylen's loafers. There was a set of prints on one side of the gate but none on the other. "That fucking gringo!"

Through the heaviest and deepest and hottest silence he'd ever experienced, the voice of one of his friends came: "Pancho, let's go to the house and talk to Marisol."

Pancho started for the house but not to talk with Marisol. One of his friends raced across the fields. Another went toward Jaylen's trailer. The others waited by the truck. Pancho walked behind his house, got a bucket of arsenic, his rifle, and a box of bullets, and then started the tractor and drove back to the men in the truck, who were watching him the whole time. Pancho was thinking of nothing; his mind was like a plank board, hard, unfeeling. He saw his hands on the rifle, felt its weight, heard the sputtering belching sound from the tractor's smokestack, heard the soft muddy sucking as the tractor tires moved him nearer and nearer to his mark.

Jaylen came out just in time to get in his car and drive far enough up the road to park and witness Pancho bulldoze his partially built home. He turned the tractor and leveled the stack of lumber piled on the side. Alejandro and Marisol came out of the house. The rest of the men watched in disbelief as Pancho crushed the new fencing around Jaylen's place, upended the small trailer where Jaylen slept, and flattened the small storage building filled with supplies and fixtures; he smashed the stacks of drying adobes under the blue plastic tarp, and demolished every standing structure above ground.

He jumped off the tractor and poured the arsenic down the well. He then shot Jaylen's bull calf that had innocently roamed across the field thinking it was feeding time. He went across the road, set the sights on his rifle, and aimed at the butane cylinder tank. He shot. A small puff of smoke popped from the pipe going into the tank, and then a roar of plumed fire came up. Seconds later the tank exploded.

Pancho steadied his elbow on his knee and aimed at Jaylen, standing by the back of his car. Just as he was about to shoot, Marisol came up behind him, grabbed the rifle, and embraced him. He fell forward to the ground on knees and arms, trying to catch his breath and sobbing. "He didn't want to get his shoes dirty! He left . . . the . . ."

"I'm sorry," she cried. "I'm so sorry, so sorry, Panchito . . ." She cradled him and wept.

Alejandro approached. "The sheriff'll be coming. We'll take him to our house. He'll be safe there."

Marisol nodded. Behind Alejandro, she watched Jaylen drive away, hating him.

She waited until they had gone over the rise, then she walked across the field and entered the house. The phone was ringing. It was Adan.

"Jaylen called on his cell, he's filing criminal charges against Pancho. What the hell happened there this morning?"

"Zapata's dead," Marisol whispered.

"Oh my God," Adan cried. "Was it something—"

"He left the gate open and . . ." But she was crying too hard to finish her sentence.

Later, when Adan called Jaylen and asked him to drop the charges, Jaylen said, "It's not only criminal destruction. Your brother keeps talking about land grant rules. And I still haven't seen them. I've been told this is a land grant property, I know that supposedly there were certain stipulations to abide by, but I haven't seen the paper. I'm doing what I'm doing because I love this land. I love that place, it's what I've dreamed of since I was a kid. I want to make it my home. But if I'm ever going to be at peace, I have to see that paper that says I have to close that gate."

"There is a charter, dating back to the king of Spain, and it does—"

"I want to see the charter . . ."

Adan said, "My father used to study it for our property boundaries. It said to the cottonwood trees and the ditch, over to the mound of rocks, and back to the river is our land. And it does say you have to close the gate behind you, so your neighbor's livestock—"

Jaylen cut in, exasperation in his voice, "You've seen it, I haven't. When I bought the land I thought it was mine, I could do what I wanted with it. I wanted to break off my portion from the land grant and make it like any other piece of land. Maybe that road is mine, maybe I don't have to close the gate, maybe you don't really have the title to the land, maybe there is something else you're not telling me. Private property is what I know, Adan, I can use it any way I wish and not be wondering if I am doing something wrong. You said the road belongs to the community, that I can use only so much water, that I can use the common pasture, but it's all hearsay."

"No, it's true."

"Doesn't mean it's legal."

"You're telling me what's legal?"

"Not me, my lawyer, talk to him from now on. I'm sorry, Adan."

Adan called Marisol and told her Jaylen was taking the villagers to court, forcing them to prove they in fact had the title to the land. There had never been a need to record the titles at the county office, but as soon as Marisol found the land grant papers she would do just that. First, she had to locate them. This shouldn't be a problem, she thought, somebody in Agua Dulce had to have them, the older people would know.

"Produce the papers in court," Adan said, "and it's over sooner than it started."

The next morning, Monday, she called a general meeting at the community center to organize an official canvassing project, and for the next few weeks Marisol and others went visiting. They questioned farmers mending fences, asked the older men warming themselves by the pool hall woodstove, stood outside the Valdez Meat Market and stopped women coming out with groceries; notices appeared in the small 4-H farming paper, queries were posted at the livestock auction house, and word spread between every waitress, bartender, and drunk. After two weeks of grueling searches, and though the papers had passed through everyone's hands in the village at one time or another, no one knew who had them.

On the first day of court in the town of Socorro, Jaylen Maguire, dressed in a blue suit, and three distinguished lawyers with bulging briefcases sat at the table. Surveyors with scrolls of plot maps were seated behind them. On the other side of the courtroom were the old people from the village, with Marisol sitting by herself in a chair in front of the table. As she walked back from the judge's bench, after handing a list of names to the judge, she stared coldly at Jaylen, but despite her anger, she couldn't help but feel sad about what had happened. During the next ten days, though she couldn't return the look, she often felt his eyes on her.

One of Pancho's friends had given Marisol a note in court. It instructed her where to meet him later. During a two-hour recess, she went to where the note directed her and sat under a cottonwood tree by an abandoned, crumbling adobe house. Instead of Pancho, however, it was Jaylen who drove up. He parked and walked up through the yard and stood next to her. "You do pretty good as the town's counsel," he said. He was trying to sound upbeat but an undertone of sadness weighed down his words.

"You do pretty good betraying people." Her words were clearly bitter. "We welcome you into our community, and this is what you do."

He knelt on the ground next to her and took her shoulders. "It's a legal formality, Marisol. I love you, and I'm sorry this had to happen—this is not in any way a reflection of the love I have for you."

"Get your hands off me!" She slapped him away.

A half mile away, still hiding in a hayloft from the law, Pancho was all set to leave and see his sister when he saw a flock of crows scatter from the cottonwood tree where he had told her to meet him. He could see Jaylen and Marisol through his binoculars. As he walked back to his car and drove off, Jaylen didn't know that Pancho had been watching them the whole time.

During the next few days Marisol resumed her role in court, calling one resident after another. They all testified about how their families had originally come from Spain or Mexico—their lineages boasting famous Spanish explorers and Plains Indians—and how the land had been handed down from generation to generation to the present time. Sometimes the witnesses had to be excused to use the bathroom, or an afternoon was wasted as testimonies trailed off into long-winded stories describing heroic exploits and tragedies, even sinking to rumors about a woman's indiscretions, or scoldings of so-and-so for moving away and abandoning responsibilities, or reports of how so-and-so was a no-good loafer, but eventually, nine days after the trial had started, all the villagers between the ages of forty and ninety had told the court their stories of seeing and reading the land grant papers.

Jaylen's lawyers argued, with a hint of derision in their tone, that although the testimony was impressive and would make for a good historical story, it hardly belonged in a court of law. No one had produced the documents needed to prove ownership, and any argument based on something that clearly did not exist required no litigation at all. But in the spirit of benevolence, they were prepared to offer a plan that would help the villagers settle their confusion and insure against future mix-ups.

They petitioned the court to create a corporation of the land grant holders, giving each villager a certain number of property shares, and those who wanted to sell, could sell; others who didn't would not have to. The corporation would be run by a commission charged with soliciting members' input on issues affecting the village and with decision-making on its behalf. The judge adjourned, saying he would assess the matter and reconvene in a week, whereupon he would have a ruling.

The day after Jaylen had met Marisol out in the woods, he quit showing up for court. Marisol thought it was because of their fight and for her it was more comfortable without him in the courtroom. Now, at least, she didn't have the constant feeling that he was watching her every gesture.

The truth, however, was that on the evening of the day Jaylen had met Marisol, he had spent the last hours of daylight cleaning up the destruction Pancho had caused. Too tired to head back to his motel room miles away in Belen, he decided to nap a bit in his sleeping bag and then maybe go into town later.

In the middle of the night, he was startled awake by the click of a pistol at his right temple. "Get dressed, you sonofabitch, you're going for a ride!" Pancho's voice crackled in the dark.

He whacked Jaylen with the end of the pistol handle. "To teach you the rules around here."

Disoriented, Jaylen couldn't do anything but get dressed and leave with Pancho in his old truck. They drove out to the west mesa and the three dormant volcanoes, where Pancho had him park at the base. The volcanoes were shallow and looked almost as if a meteorite had created them. They had plenty of moonlight to see by as they climbed up to the rim and went down into the crater. They hadn't said a word between them the whole time, and not until they were standing face-to-face in the pit did Pancho say to him, "Here's where I usually target practice. Never thought I'd come here like this. Say your prayers, Jaylen. I'm only paying you back for what you did to cause Zapata's death." There were spent rifle cartridges around bullet-riddled rusty cans and old ashen campfires with logs set around them.

"You're not serious are you? You're going to shoot—" One second after getting Pancho's attention, Jaylen leaped at him and they wrestled on the ground until the gun fired several shots that ripped sharply in the night, ricocheting off the volcanic rocks in the crater. Finally, Pancho rose and stared down at Jaylen, who lay on his back with his hands on his stomach, the shirt bloody around his navel. Pancho walked over to a nearby outcropping and sat down.

"Was it worth it, Pancho? You're going to prison for the rest of your life."

"Gravedigger, I don't want you telling me anything."

"I love her and she loves me."

"She'll only love the memory of you."

"She won't forgive you, Pancho."

"I'm not asking for forgiveness. And besides, it wasn't about you and her. I had already decided, the night before, that I was going to let it go—what you and her had between you, it was going to be okay with me. Funny how it all works out sometimes. Just when things were going to be fine, because you didn't want to get your shoes dirty, your nice suit rained on, you leave the gate open!"

Jaylen saw Pancho's eyes in the moonlight. They were moist. Pancho wiped his eyes and lay back down on the rocks. Jaylen was about to say something to Pancho when he saw a white ribbon blow up from a rock crevice. The rattlesnake sidled in quick over the flat rock and struck Pancho in the upper arm. Pancho groaned and turned over just as the rattler vanished into a rock spill.

"Pancho, try to suck the poison out. Get us out of here or we're both going to die!"

Pancho gave a pained laugh. "It doesn't work that way. We're supposed to die, life sucks, it ain't worth living."

"But if you don't do something . . ."

"We'll both die, Jaylen, we'll both die . . ."

Shortly after, with the cool night breeze blowing over their faces, both men gently drifted into unconsciousness. They were too far gone to be aware of horse hooves clattering over the rocks, and they were already chilled with the onset of death when Red

Wind came upon them. He spoke to Pancho but Pancho didn't hear him.

"I heard shooting up here, thought you were target practicing in the moonlight." He looked at Jaylen's body on the ground in a soaked bloody shirt and Pancho's swollen, purple arm. "What did you do, old friend?" Red Wind asked.

Marisol had a queasy feeling in her stomach that things hadn't gone so well for the villagers, but a plan was starting to form in her mind to get Adan involved. During the following week of adjournment, on a Monday morning, she drove up to the community center and helped seven of the oldest women in the village into a gray minivan. These women—the midwife, the babysitter, their mother's three sisters, the wife of the hardware store owner, the neighbor who had cooked and sewn for them after their mother passed away—had all known Adan since he was born. It had been a long time since any of them had gotten out of the village. The women were having a great time—young girls again in spirit, laughing and joking as if they were on a school field trip. During the ride they all took turns recalling comic events they remembered in Adan's life when he was a child.

When they reached Adan's law office in Albuquerque, Marisol ran upstairs to get her brother but the secretary told her he had gone to the spa. They sat in the reception area and waited, unwrapping the tamales, burritos, and *biscochitos* they had brought to eat. When Adan finally entered the office, he was alarmed at first, then embarrassed, because his colleagues were coming and going and gawking at the old women dressed in old-fashioned country skirts, mended shoes, and head veils eating their burritos.

He wanted to explain that he worked for a corporate law firm and you couldn't just come in and demand his time like this, but instead he said nothing and escorted them into his office.

"There something wrong?" He wrinkled his brow and his eyes paused briefly over each of their faces.

"Oh no, they just want to talk with you," Marisol said.

The women spoke up and reminded him of things he had forgotten. How Ophelia had made his lunch for years, making sure he had cinnamon cookies in his little lunch pail. How Dona Mirabel had darned his clothes and spent weeks picking out cloth and sewing his communion suit and graduation clothes. Senora Trujillo recalled the time Adan had a fever and she had nursed him for days, sleeping in a chair at his bedside, serving him soup mixed with herbs she had gathered herself. The other women remembered all the months and years when they had held bake sales to raise money for his college textbooks and travel expenses for summer seminars in Mexico, and they remembered sending him food every week during his summer jobs. The list of kind but tedious deeds went on and on—which was all to say that now, when they most needed him, he had an obligation to help. They didn't ask him, they didn't accuse him or make him feel bad or put him under duress to do something—each simply gave her story with a smile while the rest of the women nodded their assent or frowned and shook their heads in disapproval, remembering very clearly and commenting on how the weather was, what fiestas were being celebrated, who was born or had recently passed away. When finished, they cleaned up after themselves, put on their headscarves, clutched their purses, and sat in silence.

With deliberate hospitality he embraced each of them and asked them to sit in the waiting area; he needed a word with Marisol.

He sat back in his red leather captain's chair and glared at her. "Why? You know I cannot defend you, it's a conflict of interest."

"Who sold the land that was never to be sold?" she asked, then added, "It's not about that anymore, it's about the survival of the village. I don't understand how to fight them, law is confusing, it's not English or Spanish, it's a foreign language. And it's not about you or me anymore, but about all our relatives who came before us, and those who will come after."

He stared at her, not conscious of really seeing her, and went over the reasons in his mind for why he couldn't commit himself to the case. It was true, though, that the law had its own logic, and oftentimes even the worst of criminals were found innocent and those who were innocent were found guilty. In Marisol's world right and wrong were easy to discern, but the law didn't hold the same view.

"Maybe I shouldn't have come," Marisol said, rising from the chair. She felt sickened and heavy.

"I'm sorry," Adan said. "I'm willing to ask another lawyer to help you, but I can't."

"We don't want another lawyer." Marisol turned to leave.
"I'll see what I can do," he said behind her.

She had the door open, and she looked back at him. "You know what's right, Adan." She shut the door quietly behind her and left.

Marisol returned late in the afternoon and called people for a meeting, and after dinner the community center was packed with more residents than ever before—cowboys, farmers, ranch hands, laborers, homemakers, all milling about discussing the court situation and the mysterious whereabouts of the land grant papers, some people even attributing their disappearance to the evil work of witches or the dead.

Marisol stood in front, and when everyone had settled in folding chairs, she announced the bad news: Adan could not represent them. And she added that maybe it was too late anyway; their not being able to locate the land grant papers was really what it all boiled down to.

Marisol opened the meeting to the floor, and amid the general expressions of worry and men vowing to shoot anyone messing with their land, Adan came through the door, strode to the front of the community center, and set his briefcase down on the folding table.

"Today my sister came and saw me and I said I couldn't represent you because of conflict of interest. I want everyone to understand I'm not here to represent you, only to give advice, to explain to you what you're up against." He tried to sound positive but his words were flat.

"You sound like you're on their side," a defiant young man up front yelled out.

"What are you talking about?" asked a man in back with his irrigation galoshes still on.

"Do you want me to tell you the worst that could happen? The odds of winning the case are not good," Adan continued.

The oldest man in the village, Mr. Torrez, stood up leaning on his cane, and asked, "Adan, what can happen if we lose?"

"You'll probably have to file individual titles to your land. There'll be litigation in court . . . some people will say it's not your land, you won't be able to afford lawyers to prove that it is, those with the money will win . . . Developers will offer you money and some will sell. Land taxes will go up, you won't be able to afford them. Everything will change . . ."

Mr. Torrez started shaking, then clutched his chest, and collapsed. His son Johnny, a stout, brawny cowboy, sitting beside him, immediately carried his father out. Others followed and the gathering in the center dispersed. Adan stood there, feeling the worst he'd ever felt.

That evening Adan went with Marisol over to the Torrez family's small house. He and Marisol sat on the porch. They'd been up all night and it was close to dawn. During the night Mr. Torrez had passed away. A lot of people had come to pay their respects and gone, but a lot more were arriving now at daybreak. He greeted each one as they climbed the porch steps. Marisol was sipping a cup of black coffee from one of the ladies inside the house.

"I tried not to get involved but it's impossible," Adan said. "I thought I was beyond all the emotional attachments to this place but something in me stubbornly keeps worrying about their welfare. What's going to happen to them?"

"What else can happen," Marisol said with a sigh. "The thought that Torrez might lose his land killed him."

"Marisol, selling it is not the end of the world, it's the beginning of a new life."

They were quiet. The sun crested the Sangre de Cristo Mountains and spread across the valley, illuminating the cottonwoods. Crows and geese flew overhead, sparrows zipped in and out of lilac bushes big as trees, dogs, horses, cows, and sheep shook their heads and scampered and sounded their individual voices for food, workers drove their old pickups down dirt roads, mothers hurried children to the school bus stop, the air was crystalline and pure and the sky blue and the land rich with greenery, flowers, and water.

"I'm going to the chapel for a while," Marisol finally said.

Adan said, "We're in need of a miracle on this one."

Marisol got in her truck and drove down the dirt road that wound around the hills to the small church a few minutes away. She parked outside its gate, opened and closed it, and stood before the grotto of Saint Agnes. Someone had placed fresh yellow flowers in a vase at the base with a prayer card. She said a prayer and entered the old church. She knelt at a side altar, leaning her elbows against the wooden railing that skirted the altar. Banks of votive candles flickered. She'd been there for some time praying when she heard the door creak, but she didn't bother turning around because she thought it was the priest or one of the old women who came and went throughout the day.

As she prayed, her mind ranged freely over the past two months, asking the spirits to help her understand it all, pleading with God to lift the weary weight from her heart. She was still in love with Jaylen but she tried to keep him out of her mind. The accident with Pancho's horse and the subsequent court proceedings had completely thrown her off balance emotionally, and she was swept one way loving him and then the other way hating him. She lit two candles, genuflected, and turned to see Red Wind in the last pew. It startled her, and for a moment she thought he was a ghost summoned by the power of her prayer, invoked by her subconscious, and then as suddenly the spell dissipated when he rose and came toward her.

"I saw your truck outside," Red Wind said.

"Is Pancho with you?"

"No. He's at my grandfather's place, out on the res."

They sat under an apple tree on a bench behind the chapel. He told her the story about the shooting, the snakebite, and how he came upon them. In view of them a sheriff's car pulled up. A deputy in a black and tan uniform looked around. They watched him get out, answer someone at the department on his CB radio, and after a few words drive away.

"They're looking for Pancho."

Red Wind cleared his throat. "I'm sorry about the court hearings. I've got to go, but I'll come by later, when it's dark."

Marisol went back to the Torrez house and sat on the porch. She heard one of the women inside call to a young man, "Get Papa's stuff down from the attic, get his good clothes out, we have to dress him for the church viewing tomorrow."

The house was packed with mourners weeping and lighting candles and commiserating with Mrs. Torrez, who was busy feeding everyone, going back and forth to the stove and refilling the red chili bowl, bringing more rice and beans and hot tortillas and green chili salsa.

"What are you going to do about the charges?" Johnny asked Adan.

Adan was with the men in the backyard standing around a bonfire.

"I don't know what we can do," Adan said.

Alejandro said, "The judge in Belen could care less about us poor farmers. It's the ones with money they love. Pancho will stay free until they catch him, then he'll do his time. He don't give a shit, he did what he thought was right, and that sonofabitch is lucky to be walking around."

They nodded. "We go back to court tomorrow," Johnny said.

"There'll be trouble . . ." someone said.

Everyone was quiet, staring into the flames, until Johnny said, "Come on, let's find Papa's suit."

They went inside, made their way around people in the kitchen, crossed the living room packed with men smoking and sharing memories about Mr. Torrez. They tugged the rope dangling from the hallway ceiling ladder and slid it down, then climbed the stairs into the dusty attic.

"Can't believe they kept all this stuff. . ." Johnny said, opening an old cedar chest. He started to unfold a stack of ancient suits wrapped in plastic. Beside the chest Adan noticed an old leather bag with "Made in Kansas" stamped on it. He unclasped the bronze hinge and rummaged through the contents. Inside he found a bunch of old dentist's stuff—pliers, picks, molds, dentures. At the bottom was a plastic bag of photographs.

"Yeah, here's some pictures of your dad when he was young," Adan said. He pulled them out and Johnny and Alejandro shouldered up to him. They were sweating as they went through the old black-and-white photos.

"I didn't know he went to dental school in Kansas. Didn't even know he played the sax. Look at him, that's crazy, he looks cool." They stared at the photo of Mr. Torrez as a young man in a suit and fedora, holding a saxophone and smiling into the camera. The last photograph they pulled out was a large one and made crackling sounds as they unfolded it. They immediately realized that it wasn't a photograph but a sheet of yellowing parchment— the original land grant papers, obviously written with a feather quill, but still readable.

They looked at one another in shock, Adan pointing at the papers and trying to muffle his laughter. But Johnny's laughter bellowed out and Alejandro's roared; they pursed their lips, squeezed their eyes shut trying to contain themselves, but they soon fell on each other laughing and holding their sides in pain. They broke out again and again, recovering their composure only long enough to wipe their eyes and point to the papers before erupting into another fit.

Mr. Pacheco, a dignified older man, yelled up from downstairs to have a little respect. He immediately strode up to the attic, peered into the dimly lit space, and gruffly rebuked them. "Is this the way you mourn the passing of your father, Johnny? You should be ashamed!"

Johnny tried to restrain himself but managed only to gesture toward the papers and break down again into uncontrollable giggles.

Mr. Pacheco grasped the papers and carefully held them under the dusty lightbulb. He read them slowly, and gradually his serious brown eyes began to gleam with joy and his eyebrows arched with disbelief. Then he looked up, smiling, and started to laugh. He slapped the three men on the shoulders and then slapped his knee, saying, "*Ay caramba!*" and roaring with laughter. To the horror of the mourners, all four came downstairs in a state of helpless hysterics. But when they read the papers to the gathering of grievers, the funeral turned into a party.

From tears to laughter, from sitting solemnly to dancing, the mourners drank and laughed and Mrs. Torrez assured everyone it was quite all right, saying, "He would have loved it." While the men made runs to the nearest bootlegger for beer, the women started cooking up more food.

Monday morning, Marisol proudly laid the land grant papers on the judge's desk. He read them and summarily dismissed the case. She declined the numerous dinner invitations circulating among the people gathered at the courthouse and hurried home because Red Wind had told her he might be coming in today with Pancho and Jaylen. The last time they had talked, he had said that they were recuperating fine but couldn't be moved yet. Jaylen's team of lawyers and engineers had no idea of his whereabouts, and when they asked her, she simply said that he might be coming by later and she would tell him to call them. Marisol went home and ate some crackers and peanut butter, and then walked over to Jaylen's place and looked around. She sat until late in the afternoon watching the river flow south, then she returned home and napped for an hour in the parlor.

Late that night she awoke, thinking she heard horses neighing, and went out to the barn, figuring that Pancho's horses had gotten out of the corral. She expected to see the big bay mare tearing at the orchard branches. She opened the screen door and stood on the porch, staring at a rusted, ancient res truck parked there, the radiator smoldering with steam. It sputtered and rattled as Red Wind turned it off. He got out and motioned her over to the bed of the pickup. Pancho was in the back. He rose and embraced her.

"I'm fine," he said, his arm in a sling.

"What's that?" she asked, puzzled by the bundle of blankets piled on the other cot.

"Jaylen," Pancho said. He was tied down underneath to a willow branch cot.

"Oh." She couldn't believe it and pulled back the blankets. Jaylen smiled up at her.

"Grandpa tied him down, to keep him from moving around and bleeding all over," Red Wind said.

"I'm still not feeling that good," Jaylen said.

"Let's get him inside. How are we going to do this . . ." Marisol said. She started to untie one of the knots but Pancho took out his pocketknife and cut through several of them.

"That was your good rope," Red Wind said.

"I know it was. Let's get him in the house."

The Valentine's Day Card

The nuns were always celebrating holidays. For Christmas we made paper snowflakes and snowmen, taped them to windows, and sprayed the whole scene white. For Easter we were herded into the kitchen to boil eggs and paint them, and then later we went to a park and had our egg hunt. For Halloween we cut pumpkins and sold them to outsiders, who lined up around the front of the main building and bought trunk loads full. We were always engaged in some holiday enterprise to distract us from the fact that we were orphans and not like the rest of the kids in the world.

None of us would admit it though. We all told each other that we had parents and they were planning to come pick us up any day. That *any day* lasted for years sometimes but no one ever questioned it. We just believed it because we were all telling the same lies to help us believe that we really hadn't been abandoned. And I suppose I believed my own lies more than anyone else, because when Valentine's Day came and we had to make cards, I told everyone that I was making mine for my mother who was coming to visit me.

My problem was I couldn't read or write yet. I was about ten years old; I remember sitting in the back of the class scribbling unintelligible doodles on my sheets of paper and glancing out the window at the St. Mary's Grotto, watching how the sparrows landed.

Sister Rita kept looking at me and telling me to get busy and when she finally came to check on me and saw I had nothing but funny pictures—faces with exaggerated noses and bulging eyeballs and thick fleshy lips—she laughed to hide my shame. She was one of the nicer nuns. She knew that I was just learning to spell, and she suggested that I create a card for my mother by drawing one out.

She gave me glitter flakes and Elmer's glue and different colored yarns and shiny tiny stars and a new box of crayons and scissors. I went to work immediately. Everyone in the classroom, about forty kids, were making their poems rhyme with pretty-sounding words that conveyed their love for their aunts or moms or dads. Instead of a poem, I was going to draw the best card ever made, and I boasted to everyone that my card was for my mother.

I labored over that card for days. I cut perfect little angel figures and glued them on. I lined up bright blue and red beads and circled them around butterflies I had made. I even worked when class ended and the rest of the kids went out to the playground.

I was part of a group that always did fun stuff like throw flips from the monkey bars or see who could swing the highest and sail out of the swing and land the farthest. We were even in a go-cart building competition; we were making them out of old warped planks and baling wire and rusting bicycle rims. Staying in the classroom all afternoon, I missed playing baseball and basketball and even torturing the big state fair winner pig, Oscar. We used to go to the pigpen and rouse him from the mud and poke long sticks at his testicles to see his weenie come out and get hard. It was like a big red bow. We all giggled and ran away it was so embarrassing.

I was missing all this fun because I was so intent on making this Valentine's Day card for my mother. The making of it completely absorbed my day and I hardly even raised my head from the desk. I carefully etched out lines with different crayons, drew hummingbirds and roses, and traced paper cupids from a book. I filled in the empty spaces inside the card and on the covers with sparkle strings, nuts, and shells, and I even pasted pieces of real blossoms and grass and leaves around the letters *M-O-T-H-E-R.* At the end of the week we had to hand in our cards and when I did Sister Rita patted my back and said I had done a good job. She announced that the boy who created the best card would win a big box of cherry-filled chocolates and that we would all get to present the winning card to the person it had been made for.

I knew that I wouldn't win because many of the other boys had written real poems and they were long. So I wasn't too worried about it. Besides, making the card for those five days I felt like I really had a mother and that I was making one for her because she was coming to visit. It all seemed very real to me while I was constructing my card, and though I knew it was just make-believe, it was *good* make-believe because I was happier inside than I had felt in a long time.

So it came as a big surprise to me when we all rushed into the classroom Monday morning and Sister Rita announced I had won. Along with the box of cherry-filled chocolates, she gave me a first-prize ribbon. I hadn't written a poem, but every boy in the classroom thought I had and gave me a rousing five-minute standing applause; some of them even jumped on desks and yelled and hollered until Sister Rita had to get everyone settled down again.

That night, after handing out chocolates to my friends, I sat on my bunk cross-legged with a blanket on my lap and carefully picked chocolates and ate each one with great enjoyment. I felt like the luckiest kid in the world.

Then something bad happened. Since I had won for the best card, it meant I had to give the card to my mother, and I knew in my heart that my mother would probably never come to see me. That was a bad night for me, and for hours after the lights were out I kept worrying about what I was going to do, and then I came up with a good idea.

That night I waited until everyone in our dormitory was asleep and I got out of my cot and dressed and snuck out of the dorm. As soon as they found out I had no mother for real, every kid in the orphanage would laugh at me. I made my way through the cold dark to the main building, went inside, climbed up two flights of stairs to my classroom, and went in.

The moon was bright outside the windows and it made the room even quieter and colder than it was. I sniffed the playground smells of my friends lingering around the desks—

Peanut Head, Big Noodle, Cuckoo Clock, Tony Baloney. One of the radiators along the wall popped a noise and I jumped back in fright. The paper hearts and flowers taped to the windows smelled like sweet perfumed candies. A big black moth fluttered against one of the panes. I crept up to Sister Rita's desk, pulled her drawer back, and found my card right on top with a big ribbon on it that said "First Place." I took off the ribbon and tore up my card and poured the pieces into the trash can next to her desk. Then I went back to the dorm and got into bed like nothing had happened.

I didn't go to sleep right away because I kept thinking about the card and how pretty it was; I really liked it and wished I could have given it to someone. My grandma would have been perfect, but she had died over a year ago. I tried not to feel bad but I did, and so I closed my eyes and pretended I was meeting my mom in the visiting room and all the kids were there and I was handing her the card and she was crying and hugging me. I fell asleep like that.

The next morning, I acted like nothing was wrong. We dressed, went to Mass, then went to breakfast, and after chores the school bell rang and we all mobbed our way into our classrooms. We normally said a small prayer to begin the day but this morning we didn't. Sister Rita stood in front of the classroom and, almost in tears, denounced the evil perpetrator who had done such a thoughtless thing to my card. She had taken out all the scraps of torn-up card from the trash can and now she held them up in a clear sandwich bag for the class to see.

Her bottom lip was quivering when she said, "Who could dare do this! I want the person who did this to come forward!"

My head was spinning. I placed my hands on the desktop to steady myself because Sister Rita was staring at me, the other kids were glancing furtively in my direction, and all were thinking what a terrible crime it was. Then my body, carried by some power other than my own will, moved toward the front of the room. The air became opaque. I wanted to scream out something about my mother to break the horrible silence closing in on me from all sides. I was nearing Sister Rita's desk and vaguely overheard her say she was taking away all playground and recess privileges until the culprit came forth. As I started forming the words "*I . . . my . . . mother . . .*" she stopped mid-sentence and glared down at me. Then something softened over her features, and I thought she was going to cry as she took my hand and walked me outside of the classroom.

"I did it because the only mother I have," I whispered to her, "is in here," indicating the heart in my chest. "Even though I tore that card up, she still has her card." Sister Rita seemed to understand because, instead of spanking me as I expected, she knelt on the floor and hugged me.

Enemies

Chancla, Boogey, and Bomber had one thing in common—they all wanted to kill each other. None of them had had a visit in the four and a half years they had been down in the dungeon. They had no wives, no children, they didn't know where their parents were, and they hadn't seen their brothers and sisters in years. They could die tomorrow and no one would grieve them, no one would miss them, no one would even know they had lived and been on earth.

Even the prison administration had forgotten them. There were only two people who had them on their radar: the old brittle-boned tier guard who seemed on the verge of crumbling when he slowly rose from his chair in the corner to unlock their cells—once a week to give them a shower and once a week for an hour of exercise in the cage behind the dungeon—and the obese chow guard who carted in their meals—three times a day, sliding their pewter trays under the cell bars and returning an hour later to pick the trays off the landing floor where they had settled after the three convicts hurled them against the wall.

They were like three warriors from three warring clans stranded on an island who had long ago given up hope of ever rejoining their tribes or being rescued. It had been four and a half years since they had worn clothes. They rose and ate and slept and paced their cells in their boxer shorts. This was their world, day in, day out, and it never varied. Minutes crept by monotonously, and the three convicts would stare at the bars, amused by the rats racing by to snatch away morsels of the crusty leftovers stuck to the wall; by the spiders weaving cobweb after cobweb in the protective mesh screen covering the old ceiling lightbulbs. For at least one hour a day the men would stand clutching the bars of the cell, looking out on the tier, pushing their mouths into the space between the bars, and growling how they were going to kill each other.

When the warden first sent them down to the dungeon, Boogey was in the Black X gang and had already been in prison for eight years. He was twenty-nine years old, out of Georgia, and angled like a plow blade. He looked like Mike Tyson—square jaw, beady dark eyes set wide apart, shoulders brawny as a draft horse harnessed in a quarry pit. He lived with a constant craving to crush his granite cell to dust, and the fact that he could not do it caused his fury to course down from his red-clay heart through his blood vessels, intestines, and stomach. It simmered through his features and his gestures glimmered dangerously with rage in the sweltering dungeon.

Bomber was a skinhead and an expert at making bombs. The other two were constantly goading him, speculating that a bomb must have gone off in his mouth because his teeth were worse than rusty railroad spikes. He was twenty-three years old and mean as a wounded badger. But he hadn't always been this way. Once he was a big, plump-cheeked, cornbread-eating, innocent Kentucky kid with a bucktoothed smile, who spent his days out hunting and fishing. He helped his mom wash clothes in the wringer washer and hang them on the clothesline, and herded his six siblings safely along the creek to school and back. Now, in the privacy of his own mind, he often wondered about the exact moment he had gone bad. Real bad. Armed robberies. Assault and battery. Murder for hire. Contracting out his services to burn buildings for insurance companies. The list went on and on, and over time his life of deception and violence had molded the very contours of his body into the unmistakable shape of crime. The vertebrae in Bomber's lanky, sinewy torso seemed to coil when he slept and then move like a rattlesnake when he woke—vanishing in an instant and reappearing to strike from behind. He had shoulder-length white hair, albino eyes, white eyelashes, and venomous tattoos on his pale skin that advertised his hatred for spics, niggers, and Jews.

Chancla, an American-born Spanish kid from Seattle, down eleven years on two counts of smuggling massive amounts of white Asian heroin, was a handsome criminal. From his neck down to his ankles he was tattooed. But his tattoos were not of vulgar symbols; they were elaborate adornments of high and low art—van Gogh's idyllic wheat fields rolled over his left shoulder and down his back; Stan James's Big Sur ocean waves lapped at his rock reef heart; an Ansel Adams's sunrise over the Grand Tetons spread across his right shoulder blade; a bar graph necklace of musical notes from Van Morrison's song, "Take My Trouble Away," hung around his neck; a Mexican marketplace brimming with fruits and folk knickknacks covered his stomach; I Ching cryptograms banded his biceps; lightning streaked down his forearms and ended in fiery talons at his knuckles; and draping his legs was a Venetian tapestry of merchants in gondolas floating serenely in a channel. When he wasn't in prison, he could get any woman he wanted with absolute certainty. Any woman Chancla's eye landed on, Chancla got. She could be married, single, of any ethnic or religious background, old or young—it didn't matter, she would fall under his strange hypnotic magic. Women adored his glossy black hair, his almond skin, his shy smile and strong white teeth, his ballet dancer's physique, and his gold earring plugs studded with rubies. Most of all they loved the quiet attention he gave them. At its truest core, his life could be understood only through the innumerable love affairs he had had. He yearned for the day when he could be free and in the arms of a woman, a thousand miles away from the prison dungeon and the monotony of daily death threats from Boogey and Bomber.

It was against the law to keep a convict in the dungeon for more than ninety days. Boogey had been placed in the dungeon by the reclassification hearing committee because he had stabbed several rival convicts. When the guards had discovered a cache of drugs and weapons during a shakedown of Bomber's cell, Bomber had received ninety days in the dungeon as punishment. Chancla was caught making love to a beautiful sixteen-year-old boy who had been tried and sentenced as an adult, and was sent down to the dungeon for ninety days. For all three men, those ninety days turned into another sentence on top of the sentence already handed down by the courts for their original offenses. In the past they had sent word to the disciplinary committee through the chow guard, arguing that the prison was committing a crime by keeping them down there, but the committee members ignored them. Illegally confined to the dungeon, with no money to pay a lawyer to fight their case, and no access to law books if they wanted to fight it themselves, they had resigned themselves to the dungeon forever.

Four and a half years without sunshine and hardly any exercise, while being constantly confined and forced to breathe the stale, rancid air, had made them more than a little mad, and every afternoon each one spewed his frustration on the others, vowing at the first opportunity to eliminate the other two. Pacing their cells day after day, season after season, they planned out their vengeance and tormented each other with detailed accounts of the horrors they would inflict and the gruesome methods they would use— dismemberment, burning, decapitation, disembowelment, perverted sexual torture, and hanging.

Of course, though they would not admit it to each other or even to themselves, in their innermost private thoughts each dreamed of leaving the dungeon and joining the general prison population back out on the yard. Each wished it was in his power to amass consecutive days of good behavior and enjoy more freedom and privilege—such as going to school, attending social activities hosted by visiting civilians, and eventually even working up to conjugal visits.

But it would never happen, because one morning Captain Morgan came down to the dungeon and announced to Boogey, Bomber, and Chancla that they were all being released, no strings attached.

The three convicts immediately thought that they were going to be sent out back behind the cell block and shot and buried. It would not have been the first time; on occasion the guards would take a convict out in the middle of the night and he would never be seen again. But even this threat to their lives didn't bring the three of them together. Instead, they snarled at each other and acted as though the second their cell gates opened they would be on their prey like a hawk on a sparrow.

The first guard came and let Chancla out. He was forced to put on clothes, which made him feel strange and vulnerable, and he was so certain that he was being taken out to be killed that he ignored Bomber and Boogey and asked the guard, "Why they letting us go?" The guard didn't answer. Chancla's paranoia grew when he was chained up at the ankles, then around the waist, and then handcuffed at the wrists. He shuffled awkwardly out of the dungeon, filled with mounting dread and despair. It was not the way he wanted to leave.

"I'm still going to kick your fucking asses," he yelled behind him as the guard unlocked the last gate and pushed him through. He heard Bomber and Boogey's voices echoing down the cavernous tier, shouting that they couldn't wait to cut him to pieces and feed him to the dogs. Their familiar voices were comforting to him and he felt sad at leaving behind the two men who wanted him dead but had become the closest thing he had to a family.

The guard walked Chancla across the yard, posted him next to the processing office, and ordered him to wait. Though he was chained and helpless, Chancla stood nervously darting his head around, ready as he could be to hobble away from the assailant he knew was lurking there. He determined that he could at least bite the guy and chew off his nose or ear, before he was shot to death.

Back in the dungeon, Bomber pushed aside his locker and started digging frantically in the wall for his shank, a six-inch homemade steel knife that he kept hidden inside a hollowed-out brick. He brandished it before the guard, yelling, "Come get me and I'll cut your stinking rat-faced fat neck, you dirty bastard." The guard knew that without the bars between them, Bomber would surely sink the blade to the hilt without batting an eyelid. He radioed for reinforcements and four other guards arrived, all wielding bulletproof Plexiglas shields, clubs, and mace. They forcibly subdued Bomber, shackled him from ankles to wrists, dragged him out across the yard, and stood him next to Chancla.

Even though they could hardly lift a finger, Bomber and Chancla lunged at each other. Guards yanked on their chain leashes and pulled them apart, but they still kept snarling and threatening to kill each other the instant the chains were removed. In the midst of their skirmish three guards pushed Boogey toward the other two, who started in on him, cursing him and vowing to dismantle him bone by bone. Of course, Boogey retaliated by charging them. The guards standing by grew so annoyed at their relentless antagonism that they kicked the feet out from all three and made them sit on the dirt. Every time one of the convicts ranted out obscenities at one of the others, a guard slapped him across the face with a lead-filled thong.

Behind all their snarling and lunging and cursing, each felt the fear of a man walking down the death row corridor to the electric chair. Except, in their case, death was most likely to happen out on some forlorn prairie while they stood and looked at the weeds and cacti and sage, waiting to be devoured by the ants, coyotes, and buzzards.

The guards led them through various gates and when they were finally outside, beyond the walls, each vaguely recalled his arrival, being intimidated by the guard towers, the looming fifty-foot wall of granite topped with tangled rolls of fanged security wire, the floodlights, the catwalks, and the guards cradling M16s as they patrolled the perimeters.

Now here they were outside the walls just as dawn was breaking, with thoughts of imminent death darkening their hearts. Flanked by two guards apiece, they hobbled to a van waiting in the semidarkness and were helped in and separated from each other. The driver took them down a long entrance lined with palm trees, then turned left toward the airport, leaving the prison behind in the distance.

The convicts fell quiet as they stared at their reflections in the black glass, recognizing bitterly that youth was leaving them, and that they had grown old, not in flesh or physique, but emotionally, spiritually. Their eyes scanned the surrounding prairie. It was like seeing a new land. They meditated on who they had been, what their lives had been like when they were free. Now they felt more imprisoned than ever by their own fears. What were they going to do? They didn't know how to be fathers and husbands. Where were they going? If they lived, by what means would they survive? They had no money, no jobs, no schooling. Yes, they were leaving behind the prison but not what prison had done to them—criminalized them, made them meaner, crueler, and angrier.

They drove on, somewhat relaxed by the humming engine, as the lights inside homes across the road flickered on, cars backed out of driveways, and kids boarded yellow school buses.

Each one regretted that such mundane activities had eluded them for so long. They had been looking for excitement and adventure and had been swooped up early in life by the delusions of the gambler, who thinks he can win it all and be happy and rich—if only he could make one big score, do one good deal, meet one wealthy woman. These were the absurd dreams of the foolish young boys they had been, dreams that were now eaten away like apple cores thrown out of a window for the crows to peck into pulp.

When they finally arrived at the airport, their nostalgia had reawakened their hurt and their hurt had made them angry. They burned with shame when the guards led them into the terminal and stood them in the lobby for all the travelers to glare at. The guards first unlocked their wrists, then handed each of them forty bucks and a one-way ticket to his respective home state, along with a manila folder containing their release papers.

"You gonna tell us now why you're setting us free?" Boogey asked.

"Class-action suit was filed by one of the jailhouse lawyers on behalf of two hundred of you assholes. AIDS and Hepatitis-C convicts pardoned by the governor for some law called deliberate indifference. We tried to kill you infected queers off, but one of you went and filed a lawsuit. Others had their sentences commuted and they were released."

"Where do we fit in on all that?" Bomber asked.

"Given your good time, you all would have been out a year ago. Apparently," the guard said, "you guys had finished your sentences and were just doing free time. According to the courts, that's cruel and unusual punishment—all right, I'm going to unchain you and you better fucking wait until we leave the terminal to attack each other or we will take you all out back and fuck you up."

The men were so shocked by the news and so completely out of their element that they were virtually paralyzed. Swiftly abducted in the middle of the night, shoved into a van, and deposited among hundreds of strangers from all walks of life coming and going—what could they make of it? From the dungeon, with its lack of sunlight and sensory stimulation, where they had no access to radio or TV and were kept in absolute isolation in every sense of the word, they were suddenly dumped among people hurrying by with cell phones, laptops, and DVDs, among terrorist security checks and scores of guards carrying machine guns all around. They stood speechless and scared, clutching their release papers. They looked at the money in their palms and tucked away their airline tickets. They felt dangerously exposed.

They didn't know what words to use, what feelings to have, or how to behave. They were agonizingly aware of themselves and how much they didn't belong. They saw people shake hands, embrace, kiss—societal customs that could get you killed in prison. They put one foot in front of the other in a small semicircle, looking up at the vast ceilings and gawking at the people. The security guards kept frowning at them, and they noticed that reinforcements were now hovering about the edges of the terminal. Chancla said with disgust, "I'd fuck them bitches if they were inside."

Boogey spotted two uniformed security guards entering, and as they positioned themselves against a nearby wall by a rental car booth, he smiled at them and said, "They're cute little bitches, ain't they . . ."

"You muthafucking nigger, don't you ever talk that way to white men . . ." Bomber said.

Boogey turned and snarled, "Fuck you, hillbilly bitch!"

"Yeah, and fuck you both, assholes," Chancla interrupted, looking off toward a corner of the terminal where a neon martini glass flashed in a tinted window.

The other two followed him over.

They sat at the bar, four swivel stools between them, all staring at the mirror and the line of labels on the whiskey bottles. When Chancla ordered his tequila and the bartender turned his back to reach for the bottle, Chancla reached over the counter and grabbed a knife and pocketed it. Boogey and Bomber followed suit.

Bomber looked over at Boogey and said, "Think you getting the jump on me—you're dead, you little overcooked spic!"

"And when I get done with you two, I'm go' have me a good time with yo mommas," Boogey said.

The bartender glanced furtively at them. Other customers sitting at the small tables around the counter were conscious of the three men; something about them was odd, yet they made efforts not to stare. From years of forced abstinence, their first shots had them feeling good. Boogey ordered another shot of gin, Bomber another Wild Turkey, and Chancla another tequila.

"You keep looking at us funny, you'll be looking out of the side of your neck," Bomber said to the bartender, who went red with fear and nodded and put himself as far away from them as possible, wiping the small tables and chatting with the occupants at the end of the bar.

Boogey got up and turned on the TV bracketed to the ceiling. He sat with his neck craned, making soft clicks with his tongue every time the newscaster reported another of a long list of crime stories. He toasted each crime story, saying, "Ya ain't seen shit yet . . ." He took a white plastic fork and combed his kinky hair. He grabbed handfuls of peanuts and stuffed them into his mouth, then slugged down his gin to clean the salty taste from his mouth.

"You niggers like peanuts, like monkeys," Bomber ridiculed him, squishing red cherries between his black teeth, red juice running down the corners of his mouth and his chin.

"And you crackers is all about cherries, and popping yo white-ass cherry is what I'm planning to do."

Bomber got mad at the last statement, his left eyelid fluttering uncontrollably as he swigged from the Wild Turkey bottle, picking at the label, squinting his eyes at himself in the mirror beyond the bar counter. "What the fuck you looking at, grease ball?" he said to Chancla.

Chancla had been staring in the big mirror too but was not conscious of seeing Bomber because he was deep in thought. "I've never killed anybody I didn't have a good reason to kill, and I'm thinking about the reason I'm going to kill you two," he said aloud. He got up and raised his shirt. Facing the other men he traced a long scar hidden in the lush fruit bins and said, "This punk tried using a machete—I gutted him with his blade." Pointing to a variety of other scars of various lengths and widths, he said, "Here I gave him a free shot—I fucked his wife and told him to take a free shot—he did—then I showed him how to really use it." He turned his right fist to the customers. "Got teeth stuck in these knuckles—a policeman tried to stop me from taking his car. Every knuckle had one of his teeth embedded in it. They had to wire these knuckles up—"

"What'd you do to me?" Boogey interrupted. "I kinda was trying to figure that out."

They stared at each other for a long time, oblivious of the airport activity in the background: porters in blue uniforms hurrying dollies full of suitcases; harried parents trying to keep their kids from roaming off; weeping girlfriends kissing their lovers; stern-faced businessmen and women rushing by with briefcases; unwashed, uncombed college kids with strained looks from partying the night before checking their pockets for lost tickets or misplaced IDs.

The commotion made Chancla feel more isolated than he felt in the dungeon. He had tickets to fly back home, but back home was where they had arrested him and sent him to the federal prison in Texas, then transferred him to Arizona for two escapes. Back home was Seattle, but no one and nothing was waiting for him there. He figured that as soon as he got off the plane, he'd roam around town looking for his old crime partner, and if no business came his way, he'd flip a coin to see which way to go—heads, he'd pack it to Mexico; tails, to Canada. He sat back on the stool, licked the top of his hand, sprinkled a dash of salt on it, kicked back a shot of his tequila, bit into the lime wedge, and licked the salt from his hand. "Fuck all of you," he said to the clientele glancing at him. He spun himself around on the stool and stopped suddenly, facing the mirror.

"It's that place . . ." he said to their reflections. "That place . . ."

"Fuck that hellhole," Bomber growled, now quite drunk. "Fuck that place and fuck home and fuck my wife and fuck my kids . . ." he slurred and downed another shot of Wild Turkey.

"I guess it does something to you, 'cuz I can't remember anything you did to me that I should kill you for," Boogey said.

"That place runs on us hating each other, on us killing each other—it breeds racism and it breeds criminals," Bomber said.

"Here's to that, brother." Boogey raised his glass of gin and swallowed hard.

They heard the airport intercom loudly announce a flight to New Hampshire.

"What's your flight number, Bomber?" Chancla asked, but Bomber was mumbling to himself. Chancla rose, checked Bomber's ticket lying on the counter, and said, "That was your flight they just called on the intercom, Bomber. Be good to get back home to your old lady, your kids, fish some of those streams and—"

"Fuck my old lady, fuck my home, I ain't going to nowhere except back out there to rob me some dumb muthafucka . . ." He grinned drunkenly, swiveled around on his stool, and yelled at the few travelers having a drink and minding their own business.

"Flight-number this, you cocksuckers!"

They looked up from their books and papers and prepared to leave.

"You ain't no man," Bomber heard a voice say. He turned to his left, ready to stab the fool, when he saw it was Chancla.

"So you ready to have it out now? I'll teach you who a man is, boy," Bomber retorted. He was drunk and unsteady enough that he could only stagger to his right slightly, giving Chancla the advantage. Chancla grabbed him from behind, braced his arm around Bomber's neck, and whispered into his ear, "A man, a real man, not some wipe-ass bitch, would get on his plane and make it home to his family in time for supper. A sniveling ass bitch who can't hold her liquor would pussy up and stay here."

Then Chancla pulled in tight to hold him as he struggled to free himself, flailing his knife around at the air before him but not near enough for Chancla to be in danger. Chancla looked at Boogey, who understood what was happening and nodded back to him, giving Chancla a silent signal that he was on standby, waiting for him to indicate when he was needed.

"You a man, muthafucka," Chancla continued, "you'll make it to the gate—get up on that stairway to the plane and don't let them know you're drunk—that's a man—pull it off, I challenge you."

"I'll show you, asshole." Bomber's words distorted into a lot of rolling *r* sounds as he lunged forward toward the escalators that went up to the gates.

Boogey caught him under the armpit on one side and Chancla grabbed him on the other, and they kept moving him forward, moving him fast down the corridor to his gate. Just before they reached the door, Chancla shoved Bomber against the wall, slipped his knife out of his pocket, and whispered fiercely, an inch from his face, "You gotta make it across the tarmac and up those stairs, Bomber—then you'll prove you're a man to me. And I'll respect you as a man—across the tarmac, up the stairs—you can't let them know you're drunk—do it, Bomber—"

"Do it, Bomber," Boogey pitched in.

Somehow, Bomber seemed to grasp the importance of going home and of proving to them he could handle any challenge. He gave each of them a sweeping glance, lacking any malice and showing a hint of acknowledgment that they had gone through and survived a war together. He turned and walked out into the bright sunshine as Chancla and Boogey watched through the plate glass windows. They saw him tip slightly but regain his balance, grip the stairway railing, and slowly climb up the steep steps to the door of the plane, where he handed his ticket to the stewardess. Before he vanished into the cabin, he turned and saluted his two friends, grinned, flipped them off, and disappeared into the plane.

Chancla turned to Boogey and said, "I gotta find my gate . . ."

Neither knew what to say or how to say it.

Finally Boogey said, "Uh, uh, how, I mean, how can I get in touch with you? I mean, if you want." An undertone of sadness shaded his words. He shuffled.

"Sure I want, Boogey . . ." Chancla said, and his words were pained, as if each were a thorn pulled from his tongue. ". . . Never thought anyone would want to get in touch with me though. I don't know how to write and I ain't got no number. I know— if you're in Seattle, or you want to leave a message for me, call Andrei's—it's a bar I'll probably be hanging out at for a while until I decide what I'm going to do."

"I'm in Atlanta, my momma's name is Ruby Pass . . . I'll take you fishing for catfish like you never dreamed," Boogey said.

There was an awkward moment, and when Boogey leaned forward to give Chancla a hug, Chancla involuntarily drew back, defensively, and Boogey caught himself.

Chancla said, "I didn't mean to, I just—it's weird, you know—" He extended his hands out and they slapped palms and high-fived.

Mother's Ashes

One afternoon I happened to be standing in an open garage bay when a pack of bikers descended on the premises like a storm of dark rumbling clouds. I was watching Big Joe tune up my old '52 Harley, hoisted on the hydraulic forklift, when they roared in with their hot-blue chrome pipes, smelling of motor oil and rank with road grit. There were no women with them.

Big Joe, a bearded, long-haired, six-foot-seven, four-hundred-pound giant, had been president of the biker gang Border Bounty Hunters until he retired a few years ago; high in the rafters on the wall, his gang jacket hung in a dirty glass case like an ancient collegiate championship pennant from his glory days.

Big Joe gave them a quick glance and kept adjusting the air intake screws on the '52 carb as they swarmed into his garage bay, grabbed tools from his chest, and started working on their bikes, all of which had secret compartments for carrying illegal substances.

On the surface, the junkyard operated legally, specializing in building custom Harleys for bikers, but the real bank stacker was making and selling large quantities of crystal meth, which Big Joe had been expertly brewing for over three decades. Bikers traveling from state to state regularly stopped in to have their bikes worked on and their brains retorched. So while they were tightening bolts on their Shovelhead A-frames and checking air pressure, in the shadowy recesses of the warehouse, bubbling vats of chemicals were becoming monstrous jet fuel concoctions powerful enough to raise the dead.

I was aware that the bikers who frequented Big Joe's garage were on runs, picking up or delivering something, and invariably one or two in the pack had his gruesome face thumb-tacked all over the country's post offices by the FBI—wanted for murder or for the sale and manufacture of meth. They were a scary bunch, grubby and sun-chafed, mean-tempered and saddle sore, curse-spitting sleeveless pirates who sported tattoos and gang colors.

Shortly after their arrival, a dark-haired woman pulled into the yard driving a one-ton dually, half sanded and primered. She threw Big Joe a conspiratorial look and slid past the swing door into his private quarters adjacent to the bay.

Big Joe suggested we take a break and I followed him into his office. I was not about to be left alone with the bikers. Tania was sitting in one of the three grimy office chairs with wheels, puffing on a cigarette. She wore skimpy, cutoff jeans that barely covered her crotch, a soiled plaid woodchopper's shirt that showed off ample cleavage and reeked of gasoline, and black steel-tipped boots. There was a drug-worn, unhealthy pallor to her skin and an anesthetized glassiness to her sleepless stare; her hands were blackened and chapped from working on engines, and she had an overall roughness that gave me the impression she'd be deliciously wild in bed.

We snorted up four-inch-long lines of meth laid out on a knife-sharpening whetstone, and leaned back in our salvage yard chairs. They talked about the latest news in the underworld of drugs, and as their voices droned in my ears, I imagined Tania's long brown legs wrapping around my waist. As a lawyer who mostly represents clients accused of crimes, I have learned how to take advantage of people. Many of my female clients were poor, and they wound up trading an hour of sex with me for their freedom—not a bad deal, I would say.

I was sitting there trying to figure out a way of entering the conversation and taking control so I could maneuver myself into spending the evening with this woman, when the conversation turned to another woman, Carmen, who had previously been Tania's roommate. Apparently biker informants on the street had discovered that Carmen was working with the narcs, doing buys with a wire on her; after a buy, the drug squad would raid the house and arrest the bikers. The bikers had put out a contract on her. As I listened quietly from my chair, I realized, though I hadn't seen her in years, I knew Carmen quite well, and she was one woman who had slipped through the net.

I first met Carmen after her parents were killed in an auto accident. I had been appointed executor of their estate because their will was kept in trust at our firm. During our initial encounter in my office, Carmen's erotic gestures and dancer's nimbleness immediately put me in a sweltering fever, and later we began to meet for drinks. I pretended the meetings were for counseling her on how to invest her money. Carmen looked like a Vegas showgirl, a big glamorous woman, and I could tell from the erotic, acid smell of her perspiration that she was ready to have sex with me—but it never happened. Many times during sex with my wife I've imagined that it was Carmen I was with.

I told Big Joe that I was acquainted with her, and she seemed to be a nice woman—not at all a narc—and in fact I was a friend of hers. They both stared at me for a long second, as if determining my worth. In order to dispel any suspicions they might have about my loyalty to Big Joe and the bikers, I said that I would find out whether Carmen was working for the cops or not. Big Joe nodded and the woman gave me Carmen's phone number.

Big Joe knew about my addiction to sex and knew how to feed it. A few lines of good crank is like swallowing a jar of hundred-milligram Viagras, and women on it absolutely go crazy in bed. Many times when I've been with a woman I've driven to Big Joe's to get a small amount for the night. Big Joe supplied me because he was still paying me back for a favor I did him a little over nine years ago when we first met. At the time, I was with another legal firm practicing criminal law. Thanks to some people I met through NAFTA, I was able to arrange to break his old lady out of a Mexican prison in Chihuahua, and shortly after that, I helped him come up with the seventy-five grand and legal expertise he needed to beat a drug rap—for possession of thirty kilos of crystal meth. He didn't have enough to cover my bill, so he gave me his prized '52 hog and a lifetime supply of "aphrodisiacs."

As soon as I left Big Joe's junkyard, I called Carmen on my mobile phone from the road. We met in a café on Main Street the next day. She denied she was working for the narcs and then admitted she had only done it a few times. I knew she was lying; I also knew she was high on meth from the agitated way she licked her lips and her brown eyes darted back and forth from strangers on the street and back to me. I explained that I had enough influence with the bikers to lift the contract, and all I wanted in return was a few dates. She agreed, took my hands and clutched them, and smiled, promising me everything in that smile. Then she told me her side of the story.

"It was all his fault," she began, lighting up another cigarette.

As she talked, I couldn't help but be curious again about what kind of lover she was. She was built the way I like a woman—nice farm hips with a firm cowgirl's ass, long dancer's legs, narrow shoulders with firm breasts that leaped up when she walked. She had Mediterranean features, arched eyebrows, fleshy lips, and inquisitive flashing brown eyes that drew me in.

I knew I had clients waiting for me at court, but it wasn't the first time I had been in dereliction of my duty. I love women, plain and simple, and I have gone to bizarre extremes to conquer them. In pursuit of sex I have lost homes, businesses, lots of money, and, during a couple of occasions when I was caught and shot at by enraged husbands, almost my life. My need for sex was so compelling that on the day I drove my wife from the hospital after our baby was born, I stopped by to see a client who lived on the same road as us. His wife was home alone, and with my wife in the idling car only ten feet away on the other side of the wall, I fucked her on the doorstep.

As distracted as I was by Carmen's physical magnetism, I forced myself to listen to her story.

"Oh, you've got no idea what I've been through. You remember what was in my parents' will—I ended up with almost a million dollars. My brother almost three million."

Carmen was only sixteen and her brother Michael nineteen at the time we were divvying up the estate. The two received not only the lion's share of the insurance policy money, but six houses, two four-plexes, a box of valuable old coins, and quite a portfolio of stocks and bonds.

"I hate that sonofabitch brother of mine," she fumed. "I couldn't deal with what happened to my parents but I pretended I could. I got married, had a baby, had more money than I knew what to do with, and so I got into drugs. Cocaine. Lots of it. And who do you think invested much of his money into drugs, women, and gambling? Fast cars, the high life, one day in Vegas, the next on the Riviera? Michael. It got so bad with me I gave him everything in exchange for a steady supply of cocaine. He said he was going to watch over my inheritance so that I wouldn't lose it. But at some point he said if I wanted more cocaine from him, I'd have to sign him my share of the properties, which I did. When I went through my inheritance, I still wanted more cocaine, but he cut me off. I started prostituting on the streets. Bartending at rodeo bars. Sucking dick and fucking in the bathroom or an alley for a dime bag of cocaine. I was homeless. That's when I started working for the narcs busting nickel-and-dime dealers. The narcs gave me enough to keep my habit going. And it was also legal with them to do all the drugs I wanted."

I wanted to ask her about the fucking, to describe it in detail, but I was also repulsed by the thought of the men in that sewer sludge world, where even the best of drug users have the ethical standards of roadkill. Also, I was getting irritated, sitting there pretending to care about her problems instead of attending to my clients, enduring her miserable lament on life in the hopes of getting her to fuck me.

She swore she harbored no ill will toward her brother, but I sensed she still didn't want to admit that she envied him. She stated with deep sincerity that she was now morally superior to that "human trash bin" and completely removed from "that world." She even pretended, quite convincingly, that she was on the straight and narrow. Despite her insistence that she was clean, I was certain she was still using and I planned to prove it—she would have sex with me and she would do it for drugs.

From all my years as a trial lawyer, I knew all she needed was a nudge to go over the edge—and I would provide it. I was exploiting her weakness, but I was also only pushing her to her true self, to realize that it was better to admit the nature of one's pleasures—drugs, whiskey, and fucking—than to delude oneself.

I remember a time sitting in New Orleans with a friend of mine, drinking and watching paddle wheel boats go by, when a young girl, perhaps no more than thirteen or fourteen years old, came in with her mother. My friend said it was a shame to bring a girl that young into such a seedy bar, and I retorted that he was kidding himself if he thought only men in "such a seedy bar" would fuck a girl that sweet and young. Every man would if it wasn't socially prohibited. My friend accused me of wanting to destroy innocence and crush beauty. I grunted at him and told him about my experience in private school, when my math teacher took me into her classroom after school, straddled me on her desk, and fucked me. It was about power and control, and she had both. Before I left him he asked me, "To what extent will you go to fulfill your lust?"

I have never answered that question because the limits keep expanding, and I do things that surprise me. A few days after my café meeting with Carmen, with a little time to kill, I decided to drive down to her house. I smiled thinking how I had both power and control, but I grimaced with disgust when I pulled into the trailer court where she lived. I parked in front of trailer 23 and made my way around tires, broken appliances, and plastic bags of trash strewn all over the place to reach her door, which was open. She was inside lying on a torn couch in a bikini, drinking a beer and smoking a cigarette.

She got up and gave me a kiss on the cheek, said I looked like James Dean in my black suit and white shirt, and ran her hand through my hair as I eased down into an armchair. She got me a plate and spoon and I crushed and laid out a line of meth for her, hoping it would free her up enough to lead me into her bedroom, but she declined. I did the line myself, popped a beer, took a sip, and settled in. She stretched out on the couch on her belly with her butt sticking up, her hair cascading down, her legs crooked and crossed at the ankles. I stared into her cleavage, sure

I was close to having her, when—I couldn't believe it—she resumed her obsessive tirade about how her failure in life was all Michael's fault.

"You'd think that two siblings suckled from the same tit would at least have one thing in common. Every time one of his business ventures failed, he came running to me, but there was a time when I never could see wrong in him, though I knew as early as high school that the traffic lights weren't all working in that boy's head.

"After our parents died, Michael became the man of the house. He was kind of feminine from the start, but of all the things he wanted to be—can you believe it?—a gangster, more precisely, a big drug dealer was tops. I thought he was kidding me, rabbit shy as he was. I literally had to pull him away from the school hall walls, he was so afraid of people—he'd even panic during class change in high school.

"I was the one voted most likely to succeed. I was a cheerleader. But Michael? Pimply-faced and lanky, droopy hound eyes, personality as creative as a country road telephone pole. I mean, flat. I'd take him with me to parties, he'd sit up in a corner, watch me make out with my newest boyfriend, hungering for a girl to talk to worse than a puppy whining for warm milk. I'm telling you, and you'll agree with me when I tell you this, that boy is a pure miracle from hell. If I knew then what he was going to do and how he was going to turn out, I would have been the first to put a bullet in my head. Better yet, in him, much misery as he's caused the world."

I interrupted her to remind her of how I had saved her life and how she owed me. "Look, the reason I wanted to meet was to inform you that you had to stop snitching off dealers. They've let you slide this time, and they mean it too. I've represented Big Joe twice in court, and he has connections to take out anybody he wants. Both times I got him and his associates off, and that's why they're giving you this chance, through me, to walk away alive."

"I will—I will—I will—" she said, jumpy with exasperation, glancing out through the open doorway at the beautiful view of fly- and maggot-infested trash heaps, "but I've got to tell you. This tweaker's tango really begins now, meaning my brother Michael's. Mother's will—the little bastard forged a new one to replace the old and you, as the executor, never even questioned it."

She caught me off guard with this accusation. I was about to make her prove her case when she blurted out, "That griddle-hearted sonofabitch—he's much older and more experienced in cruelty than his years. Like, when we were little, if I really needed to use the bathroom, he wouldn't let me in. He did that, cut you at the knees when you were most vulnerable. When poor Mother died, what do you think Michael did? He raced to the emergency room, stripped the jewelry off her hands and the gold and diamond chains off her neck. He swore up and down during the settlement in your office that she hadn't been wearing anything, but shortly after that I saw Michael's girlfriend and she was wearing one of Mother's bracelets. That boy lies as pretty as a glazed donut on the rack. And of course I couldn't say anything, because at that time I was getting my drugs from him. He would have cut me off. From where I'm sitting it looks like I'm the one dumber than a dog.

"Mother made me and Michael swear that when she died we'd take her ashes up to a mountain peak and scatter them, and that's one promise I have to fulfill. She wanted to be free. Never thought I'd do the things I've done, but I've got to scatter her ashes up there. You know, things happen and you look back only so many times and get tired of looking back, and just let your head hang. Mine's scraping the sidewalk."

She got up, swayed her pretty behind into her bedroom, and came back holding a silver corked vase. "This is her, where she lives right now." She knelt in front of me, one hand on my knee, the other holding the vase, looking at me. She squeezed my thigh, and I swear I thought she was going to go down on me when she drew closer and asked, "I'll find out where Michael is, but can you go up there with us to scatter her ashes?"

"Can I do what—" I blurted out, taken aback by her request and annoyed that I was letting myself be drawn this far into such an absurd affair. I had no time to meddle in other people's lives, not like this anyway. "Why does it matter to you? I don't want to be blunt, but why don't you just flush her down the toilet as you have your own life?"

"I think she might curse me if I don't do this. Maybe my life is already cursed by her, and it won't change until I do this. I'm thinking this would be a good way to get my life on track, keeping my word. I want to do this, but I'm not sure I can by myself."

"You're sincere? Did you get converted or something?"

"I want to change, I'm trying to change," she said, and got up and sat on the couch again, clutching the vase in her hands between her legs. "I want Michael in on it too, kind of like a family or something. But with me and him, we'll probably fight, it won't happen. With you there, if we get in a fight, you can stop us." She paused and then asked, "Did you go to bed with my mama?"

I nodded.

"Then that's reason enough for you to help us see she gets what she wants."

I promised to be available but gave Carmen's request little regard. In truth, I expected never to see her again. I said good-bye, a little disappointed our meeting hadn't ended as it had in my X-rated fantasy, but as I drove to my office a few blocks away, I was satisfied to forget the encounter. After all, my initial urge to meet her was based on nothing more than a compulsion to make love to every beautiful woman I met—and this failed attempt could just be chalked up to some temporary testosterone disorder.

I had a pretty peaceful life. I wanted things easy and didn't need to mess it up by adding this woman's problems. A one-night stand was not worth the hassle.

I'd all but forgotten about Carmen until six months later. It was Christmas Eve and I had a group of friends over to my house. Each had brought a dish of food to share after we returned from Mass. Once everyone had arrived we put on our scarves and coats and were headed out the door when the phone rang. I normally wouldn't have answered it, but thinking it might be a friend who was running late, I picked up the receiver.

It was Carmen, and she wanted to know whether I was ready for the ritual. Her call caught me by surprise, and for a moment I found myself unable to respond. I said I was busy at the moment and told her to call later, after the holidays, but she insisted there was no time to waste. She was calling from a hospital bed, she said, and she claimed that she was going to die and that a member of her ex-husband's family had put an evil hex on her. She sounded frantic and hysterical, and asked in disjointed phrases whether I knew a priest who could perform exorcisms.

She sounded like she was back into drugs and absolutely crazy; I told her I didn't know an exorcist and, hoping to end our discussion, told her I had to leave, that I had friends waiting for me and we were on our way to Mass. She told me Michael was at her house and that all he did was sit alone in the dark staring at the wall. She wanted me to call him and invite him to the service. I remembered her story about his greed and deception, and some part of my legal training made me inquisitive, made me want to question him and find out the truth. I hung up, after promising to see her the following day, and then I dialed Michael's number.

A sheepish, meek voice answered, softer than I expected. When I asked what Michael was doing, he came right out and told me he was sitting in the dark, staring at the wall. What surprised me was how easily and openly he admitted it, as if it was the most normal thing a person could do on Christmas Eve. Feeling pity for him, I invited him along to the evening services and he stated he didn't have a ride. I detected a deep current of helplessness, and perhaps in the back of my mind I was curious about what had become of him, how he had lost all his money. I called a friend, told him where Michael lived, and he agreed to pick Michael up.

I told my friends to leave without me and that I would catch up to them after Michael came over. When he arrived, he didn't look or act the way I expected—I guess I had imagined some-one more polished. He was around thirty-eight, six feet tall, had a long neck, a small paunch, long arms that dangled at his sides, messy black hair, and brown eyes that kept darting about. I noticed right away there was something wrong with him, as if he were underwater, moving around by some strange current rather than by his own efforts. He seemed to be on sedatives; he acted disoriented and clumsy, like a boy on a hike who had lost his way. He stood almost unnoticed against my kitchen sink, envel-oped in a vulnerable quietness that one usually observes in trauma victims. I had the impression that he was a patient man and some-one who got plenty of sleep.

He was likeable, his manner submissive in an appealing and trusting way. As we drove he told me his side of the story. It was different from his sister's version of how he had squandered his inheritance and ended up penniless on the streets. In fact, it was dismally worse. He had been arrested a few times for dealing drugs, drank a bottle of cleaning fluid while in jail, was moved to a criminal asylum, and had been heavily sedated. A later diagnosis concluded he was manic-depressive and he was given medication. On his release he was under strict supervision, had to go see his caseworker twice a week and his parole officer every morning, give random urine tests, and attend group counseling for mentally disturbed felons.

Despite his medication, Michael's manner of speaking was straightforward and he didn't embellish even the smallest detail. He said his sister Carmen was a liar. She always lied about everything. She was the one who called the cops on him the times he got busted; he was trying to protect her assets, until she sold the houses and apartments out from under him to buy herself drugs; she even depleted her savings account, then stole his credit cards and emptied all his bank accounts, which contained quite a lot of money.

But as he told me this, he didn't seem bothered. With a blank face—no expressions of surprise or resentment—and in a matter-of-fact way, he told how he lost the money, admitting that he had been foolish and even stupid, but implied that life was what it was and had happened the way it happened. He spoke about his years of degeneracy and indulgence in behaviors normally considered obscene as though they were merely an amusing walk in the park on a Sunday morning. He had enjoyed the most disgusting pleasures and experienced the filthiest fantasies and he showed no regret for having done so.

After having heard both sides, I realized that Carmen and Michael loved and hated each other, though Michael felt more love than hatred. They both wanted to blame the other for their failures, but Michael understood that his condition was the result of taking too many drugs for too long. Each was probably responsible for losing their share of the inheritance. Carmen would not accept the loss though, while Michael had embraced his folly. When I asked Michael about his mother's wishes for her ashes to be dispersed at the mountaintop, he promptly concurred that it had been her wish. Then I asked him whether his father or mother had been affectionate toward him, and he said they had probably hugged him twice in his life. Again, he gave no evidence that this was at all out of the ordinary or upsetting to him.

I'm not sure how I got so entangled—maybe I felt pity or was simply being generous—but on a nice warm Saturday I found myself packing lunches and leaving with Michael and his sister to scatter ashes in the mountains.

Carmen had become thinner. I suspected she was smoking crack. Her mind was worse than ever: she was hilariously grinning one moment, then deeply morose the next; briefly upset about world affairs and a moment later sullen over her personal life; she seemed by turns panicked and overjoyed. I would be very glad when we were finished and I could say good-bye to both of them, I thought, but for the moment they evoked my

sympathy. Plus I was feeling some strange need for compensa-
tion, a karmic balancing for some of the things I had done.

As we drove east to the mountains, I tried to imagine Michael
in his new Porsche, with millions in the bank, expensive clothes,
and apartment complexes, jet-setting everywhere, gambling in
Vegas with a baby doll on each arm. I knew that's how it had
been but I just couldn't see it. Carmen sat in the back jabbering
incoherently to the vase between her lap, promising the ashes
that they would be set free and her mother's spirit appeased.

We arrived at the peak and it was a little cooler than I expected. I put on my jacket and gloves. Carmen carefully cradled
the vase in her hands and Michael looked around groggily, waiting
to be directed. There were tourists milling about, hikers and
mountain bikers on the trails, so I suggested we walk a bit to get
away from everyone. I thought it might be nice to find a place
where they could say their last farewells to their mother in private. We followed a path along the cliff for about an hour until
we found the perfect spot. There was an overhang and beyond
it the most beautiful canyons. We stood on the ridge and formed
a circle.

"Okay," I said, "you pray, then we'll toss the ashes over
the edge. That'll be enough to free her."

"That's a good idea," Carmen said; she pulled the cork off
the vase and dragged out a plastic bag. She opened it. "Now
everyone close your eyes and pray."

With my eyes shut, I heard the wind blowing through the
pine trees and birds chirping. I started to feel myself swaying in

the wind and had to open them to regain my balance. When I did, I saw that Michael had not closed his eyes but was staring out to the city below.

"I can see where we used to live, Carmen," he blurted out.

"You're supposed to be praying," she scolded him. "Okay, now we do it." She reached into the bag and cupped a handful of ashes, stepped to the edge, and scattered the black gritty dust over the air. "Now your turn," she indicated, nodding to Michael.

"I can't," he said.

"What?" she asked.

"I can't."

"You better," she ordered. She pushed him close to the edge and shoved the plastic bag into his hands.

He flung the bag over the cliff as if it were scalding his hands. It caught in some pine branches about fifty feet below.

Carmen said, "I can't believe you did that, stupid! Now she'll never be free, she's in that bag. Some deer is going to eat her, or a raccoon or something, and she'll become animal shit! Stupid!" She accosted him, yelling in his face, until I stepped between them, afraid he might fall over the cliff.

"Okay," I said, "there's nothing we can do. Maybe we say another prayer and then leave."

"No, we can't," Carmen insisted. "One of us has to climb down there and get the bag. We promised we'd release her spirit and we have to do that or we'll be haunted by her spirit and have nightmares or something worse."

"We can't climb down there," I said with astonishment. "Are you crazy?"

"You have to," she demanded.

I looked at Michael and he shrugged. I looked at her and she stared back.

"You have to," she repeated.

"Why can't you?"

"I'm on meds . . . I'd fall."

"She's not my mother and this is crazy, that's a sheer drop of at least a thousand feet."

"What the hell, then I'll do it," Carmen said and started for the edge; she crouched down and placed a foot on a branch.

I cried, "Stop!" I grabbed her and lifted her up on her feet.

"I guess I'll do it."

I stepped gingerly to the rock lip, breathed deeply, and looked down at the bag. From the ledge I could see all the canyons and tall pine trees and sharp protruding rock cliffs below. I turned around and faced Michael.

"I don't understand why you couldn't touch the damn ashes. They're not going to poison you, it's your mother. If I bring them back up you better scatter them."

He trembled with repulsion and said, "I'll try."

"That's the worst thing that could have happened," Carmen complained. "Her spirit's imprisoned forever now."

I said, "Here, hold these—last thing I need to do is lose them." I handed Michael my wallet and keys. "I'll climb down and get it." Carefully, I started to inch my way down.

I could hear Carmen above saying, "Bastard you are. I will never rest in peace, nor will she, knowing her ashes are trapped in that plastic bag."

I chose my steps cautiously, checking the firmness of rocks, roots, and branches. After what seemed like an eternity, I finally reached the bag, unsnagged it, and had it tightly in my grip. Instead of bringing it back up, I called to them, "I'm going to scatter them from here . . ."

"Sure," Carmen called down, "do whatever you want."

Her statement sounded strange somehow.

"What do you mean," I called back. I slowly opened the bag and then looked up. Michael had a glum expression, but Carmen was smiling down at me. The ashes felt coarser than I expected, and then it hit me: it was black sand.

In my confusion, I shifted my weight slightly off balance and my foot slipped and my body tilted out. To steady myself, I reached out for a branch, but it broke. Glancing up I saw Carmen open my wallet and take out the money and credit cards. I watched her take Michael's hand and lead him down the path to my car. My wallet went right past me as I fell, hurtling down ten thousand feet into the canyon below, and I realized with sad irony, she had fucked me after all.

Bull's Blood

Franklin rose early on Saturday morning, made himself a cup of coffee and toast, and after eating, went into the garage. He grabbed a box off the dwindling stack and carried it into his study. Almost three months after he and Lynn had bought their house, he hoped to finally finish unpacking, and with a mixture of relief and annoyance that this was how he was spending his Saturday morning, he began sorting through the religious statues, paperback novels, poetry books, family photographs, old tax returns, and receipts. Most of this he threw in the trash pile. Then he opened a manila envelope and smiled when he saw what it contained: a photograph showing both of them covered in blood, taken six years before, after he first met Lynn.

A year before the photograph was taken, Franklin was still married. He was hurt but not surprised when his wife informed him that she had filed for divorce. They'd been having problems for three years, and he never really had faith that he could make it work. Something inside him had given up because none of his efforts had succeeded—marital counseling, individual therapy, and other remedies all failed to improve their relationship. He was thirty-nine and played bass guitar and congas in a salsa band; at the same time that his nine-year marriage dissolved, the band disintegrated and his close friends moved away. Of the ones that remained, two killed themselves and the rest became complacent—all they wanted out of life was to have enough people for volleyball and a barbecue at the park on Sunday.

The same weekend his wife informed him she had filed, he packed his clothes in boxes, put them in his pickup, and drove away with one last sight of her in his rearview mirror: standing in the yard, a glazed rage in her eyes and a scowl on her face. He left her everything—house, car, furniture, and appliances. He knew that he would never marry again because it would inevitably end for some horrible reason—something unseen, unplanned, but lurking there in the dark, in the near future, waiting for the right time to spring out at him and shatter his trust.

He never fully understood why his marriage soured, but he tried to accept that that's how life was: One day the good things—commitment, laughter, love, passion—were there, and the next, poof!, they were gone, leaving a residue of misery staining everything he looked at.

The work he had put into making a good life for his family never went the way it should have, and he felt that he was not good at the ups and downs of marriage, not good at sitting down and discussing what was on his wife's mind—things that mattered and which he now assumed might have salvaged his relationship.

But it wasn't in his nature to change, to take on another way of listening and acting and living, another way of caring and being with someone. He was too afraid—to wander in the dark, groping here and there, hoping his lover's hand would be there when he needed it. He could only go on as he was, and perhaps one day he and his wife could sit across from each other at a table in a coffee shop and simply talk, two acquaintances with mutual respect. He didn't believe in happiness but he could settle for stability, an unchanging continuum with no surprises.

But Franklin underestimated the damage the breakup would do to him. He rented a second-floor, two-room apartment downtown, with sliding doors on a balcony that opened to a park across the street, and while his ex-wife traveled and vacationed as if she were free and sixteen again, he spent his days listlessly pacing from one room to the other, leaning his elbows on the balcony railing, watching couples and retirees walk their dogs and come and go in the park until it was late and he went to sleep on his futon mattress on the floor.

He felt incapable of stepping outside his door and engaging anyone on any level for any reason. Over the next few weeks he became more isolated and grew increasingly bereft and melancholy.

On the day Franklin turned forty, he found himself reviewing his life. He bleakly admitted to himself that it amounted to very little. Like his former friends' lives, his was mediocre at best, and now he felt pulled down by an undertow of despair. He thought briefly about going to night school for computer programming, accounting, or real estate, but persistent inertia paralyzed him—something deep inside him was growing more and more afraid. He was falling apart, and how deep into the abyss he was going to nosedive he didn't know.

★　★　★

Six months before he met Lynn, he had closed himself in his apartment and started drinking gin and experimenting with drugs. He began to have thoughts of killing himself. He was haunted by the possibility that his life would always be like this, and the razor-sharp slivers of fear punctured the edges of his mind at all hours, intruding into his dreams and thoughts as he looked at people passing below his balcony or heard them step ponderously in the hallway past his door. He had even called his dealer to ask him to bring over a pistol along with his next delivery. He later eyed the pistol lying on the coffee table, luring him to try the ultimate high; he guessed that if he got drunk or high enough, the odds of his taking his own life were better than fifty–fifty.

He abandoned basic hygiene and walked around in boxers and a T-shirt, unshaved and unwashed. His attempt at socializing was to drink every night at the corner bar, and he became a prolific womanizer. He wanted to enjoy as many women in as many ways as possible and not think about where his life was going or how it might end. One young prostitute believed he had been bewitched and that evil spirits inhabited him, and he believed her but could do nothing about it. He resigned himself to living under the pall of damnation. To his mind, this was justification for his ongoing self-destruction.

★　★　★

Perhaps because of the elevation or from the fatigue after having driven twelve hundred miles from New Mexico to Salt Lake City, the beer hit Franklin harder than usual. He was on his sixth cup, sitting in the arena next to his cousin Louis, who had been eliminated earlier in the saddle bronc category at the Salt Lake City national rodeo finals.

A huge theater screen suspended from the coliseum ceiling flashed the next event: the women's barrel racing finals. The screen showed the contestants—pretty, ponytailed blond and brunette cowgirls with strong, sensuous, compact bodies.

Franklin didn't expect to be enjoying himself, but now that he was here he silently thanked his cousin, who had forced him to come. A few days before, Louis had run into Franklin's exwife at the grocery store, and she told him about Franklin's bizarre behavior—his refusal to answer the door or the telephone, the boozing, the womanizing, the drugs—his overall descent into hell. Later Louis went over to Franklin's, without even inquiring whether he wanted company, and ordered, "You're going to get some fresh air, see some pretty women, and party with me—get your stuff, we're leaving."

Before Franklin could make a sound, Louis choked off any protest with a forearm under Franklin's chin, pinning him against the wall, commanding, "I'm inviting you to a party, and I don't aim to be turned down by family. Get on it now 'fore I put a boot up that ass!"

At the rodeo, Franklin couldn't help but smile as he watched Louis get crushed like a bag of potato chips by a crazed, man-killing bull and, in another competition, stamped in the dust by a red-eyed bucking bronc. To witness healthy men and women, seemingly of sound mind, put their lives on the line for eight seconds gave him a reprieve from his own self-destructive habits and pulled him out of his dark mood. As he saw it, they were even crazier than he was.

There were reporters on the bleachers all around him with rucksacks filled with notepads, tape recorders, and cameras, sipping from whiskey flasks, putting the previous days' interview notes in order. Tilting his head back to gulp the last swig of beer from his paper cup, out of the corner of his eye Franklin saw a woman's face flash across the giant movie screen that hung from the coliseum canopy. At first he thought his eyes were playing tricks on him. The cup fell out of his hand, beer dribbled from the corners of his lips, and he coughed on the liquid that went down his windpipe. Regaining his composure. he wiped his eyes and mouth and studied the screen, but the woman was gone. He must have only imagined, for an instant, the most beautiful woman he'd ever seen.

The halftime show started and two cowboys drove trucks with horse trailers into the arena. A cow trotted out from one of the chutes, its milk bag flopping to its gait. A referee whistled and the two cowboys jumped out of their pickups, took out their horses, and saddled them. The first cowboy to successfully mount his horse, lasso the cow, fill a cup with milk, get back on his horse, and race to the finish line, still holding the cup of milk, won. The race took place and then the clowns came out, chasing a

Shetland pony with a blue heeler riding it. Some dove at the Shetland while others somersaulted over it. The clowns were ex–bronc riders who couldn't ride anymore because of injuries but still wanted to stay in the scene.

A little later, a tractor flanked by young 4-H cowboys came out and raked the arena smooth. They set up orange drums for the barrel racing competition and departed. A few minutes later, the first horse burst out of the gates and churned around the barrels, hooves spitting dirt puffs. Franklin was amazed at how far down these women riders could lean their horses—a mere five or six inches off the ground—while going that fast around a barrel. He saw the horses wrench sideways, snorting, every muscle strained taut to its limit. He watched in awe as rider after rider blasted out of the gate, determined to be the best.

Then the last young rider, with long walnut-colored hair, flew out of the gate. He looked up at the screen and his lower lip trembled, perspiration beaded his forehead, and he found it difficult to breathe—he hadn't imagined her after all. She was the same woman he had seen flash by on the screen earlier, and now she took his breath away.

Six years later, as he looked at the photograph he held in his hands, the sight of her bloody face looking up at him still pierced him with its openhearted vow, innocent and truthful as rays of light radiating over water at sunrise.

The initial sight of her had reignited something in him that had died, and it came alive as hot as the blinding camera flashes that flickered from the bleachers that day. All the qualities in a woman that he desired—indeed, fantasized about—he sensed she possessed. He had dreamed of her but had never pictured her face. She was more beautiful than he could have imagined.

As she flew among the barrels, strands of her dark hair flew back with the horse's auburn mane, her tanned almond complexion blended in with the horse's dark coat, and its turquoise halter, reins, and saddle trim merged with her blue eyes. She lost her cowboy hat on the first turn. Like a general charging into battle, she attacked the barrels, at times leaning so low on the turns that her reins grazed the ground. Franklin had never experienced such desire for any woman, and watching her performance on the edge of his seat, he joined the crowd to roar her on.

The times were announced immediately after each run, and after hers the announcer stated that five seconds had been subtracted from her overall time as a penalty for knocking down a barrel. It was enough to drop her to fourth. He saw her walking to the rear of the coliseum where the horses were stalled, watching closely to see if anyone met her. She was alone. Franklin hurried down the stands. He spotted her heading to the open-air stalls, and as he neared her, he started worrying that she would think he was a nut. But what could he do?

And then suddenly he was beside her, gulping for air. The sight of her big blue eyes, high cheekbones, and shapely lips stunned him almost speechless.

She glanced at him suspiciously and said, "Can I help you with something?" Her voice sounded light and yet powerful. He struggled to make himself relevant.

"No, no, well, yes . . . uhh—Lynn, right?—you did great . . ." Franklin said.

"Yeah, he did okay," she said, petting her horse, "it was my leg that knocked over the barrel." Her horse was beautiful— a black gelding, half quarter horse, half thoroughbred, it had four white stockings and a blaze of white down its face.

All around them penned-up livestock bellowed, whinnied, and bleated, and the humid air reeked of dung and horse sweat. Yet, because he was gazing at Lynn, to Franklin the encounter seemed as sweetly romantic as a snowy evening in a mountain cabin.

Lynn faced him with dust-caked cheeks, streaked where she had wiped away her tears. "What is it you want?" she asked, making an effort to sound cheerful.

"Five seconds, that's all you lost by. But you were the best . . . the very best."

She searched his face. "My horse might be poor, but he did good, it was my fault." She flushed with emotion and it took all her composure to keep from weeping.

"Can I walk back with you?" He paused. "This might sound crazy, but when I saw you, a part of me remembered you, as if you were someone I had known for a long time."

She gave him a long look as if to determine whether she could trust him. "Sure; right now I feel like the loneliest cowgirl in this whole rodeo."

★ ★ ★

Lynn called his hotel the following morning and they went out for breakfast. She had no expectations, but when she saw Franklin leaning against the red brick restaurant a sparkling sensation overcame her. As she crossed the street, though it was a warm April day, snowflakes started to float down softly. Later, when she was alone and thoughtful, she would interpret the snowfall as a heavenly omen in their favor.

From that moment on they could hardly stand being apart. They felt a history not yet lived awaiting them. And this certainty expanded and brimmed in all their senses, like the fragrant aroma of homemade bread just pulled from a brick oven. Days and nights blurred by. They gradually put their past lives behind them and in a short while it seemed they hardly even recognized who they had been, as if they had been wearing costumes until then, pretending to be people they were not.

Still, there were times when Lynn agonized over what people said and thought about them: She was twenty years old, he was forty; she was white, he was Hispanic; he was Catholic, she was Mormon, and she'd been groomed by church elders to follow the Latter Day Saints life and marry someone condoned by the church officials. When she went home to visit her parents, they threatened to disown her if she didn't come to her senses and discontinue her affair with Franklin. "He's only five years younger than I am," her father roared at the kitchen table. Her girlfriends, over drinks at the old college watering hole, guessed he was suffering a midlife crisis and advised Lynn to take advantage of it—have all the sex she wanted with him, travel, buy clothes, accept his money, then leave him. She was torn in two because she knew her parents and friends were probably right, but she loved Franklin beyond all understanding. No matter what adversity they had to face, they would take on each challenge together.

Franklin's friends were highly critical of him too; some accused him of thinking he was too good for his own kind. They mocked him for being a "coconut"—brown on the outside, white on the inside. But beyond what friends and family said, society gave the harshest condemnation.

When Lynn and Franklin relaxed in the whirlpool at the gym, women turned their contemptuous eyes on Lynn for being a young woman with an older man. In restaurants in the ski resorts north of Salt Lake City, white people glared at Franklin for daring to claim the company of a young white girl. In southern New Mexico, in cafés packed with Chicanos, customers scrutinized them and smirked, inferring that she was merely his temporary sex toy and he was a foolish man without scruples. Wherever they went in public, bigotry followed them, but in private nothing could lessen their romantic exhilaration.

Lynn had set out to get Franklin healthy again and soon had him jogging with her. They ran along the West Mesa dunes, where rattlesnakes and coyotes greeted them as they scaled the dormant volcano. He puffed and coughed and she had to wait for him to catch up, but gradually he was running next to her.

Along with juices made from fruits, vegetables, and wheat grass, she had him drink six glasses of water a day, and she fixed him robust salads. After he quit smoking, she taught him how to swim at the gym pool, and later, after swimming, they strolled along the Rio Grande, surrounded by willows, and meditated on the flowers, the flowing water, and the cranes wading in the shallows. Sometimes she would dance wildly in a clearing, captivating him in her gyrating, hypnotic mating ritual, and then they would make love on the ground.

These were emotionally packed days, grounded in a way Franklin had not enjoyed before. Being with Lynn had renewed his belief in God and given him a newfound faith in his ability to create a meaningful relationship. During this time, on the way back from a three-day camping trip, they stopped in at St. Francis Cathedral in Santa Fe. A dozen or so elderly parishioners were sitting in pews counting Hail Marys on rosaries when Franklin and Lynn entered and took a seat nearest the main altar. Franklin closed his eyes and when he opened them a few minutes later, he saw Lynn crying, overwhelmed with piety. Then she stood, went up to the communion railing, raised her arms, and began to pray aloud. The people around her stared as she thanked Christ for bringing Franklin and her together. When they left the church, Franklin asked her what had happened. Lynn said that she had had a religious experience and planned to convert to Catholicism.

They headed to a café off the plaza, and as she talked avidly about her encounter with the spirit of Christ, which she had felt infuse her being, Franklin gave a silent prayer of his own: that

God would give him the faith he needed to make the relationship work. Privately, he was still afraid love would blow up in his face again.

As summer ended they took long drives into the country, along prairie roads bordered with rolling meadows and narrow blacktop roads winding through forested mountains. During one trip Franklin told Lynn that he thought most men in their forties stopped trying to achieve the dreams they had as young men. Before he had met her, he said, he had been stuck midstream, unable to find the strength to reach the other bank, with no connections to anything worthy of belief—the spirituality movements he had sought out seemed too trendy and shallow and lacking in compassion. But now, for the first time in a long time, with Lynn's love, he possessed the strength to cross the stream and believe in people and life again.

In September the two found themselves in Washington, D.C., where Franklin had a weeklong job playing congas at a salsa club. One Saturday morning they drove to a frozen lake. Franklin picked up a large stone and threw it as far as he could onto the ice.

"I'll prove how much I love you," he told Lynn, and started out on the lake to retrieve the rock. She watched quietly with her big blue eyes tracking his every breath and step. When he finally reached the rock and picked it up, the ice began cracking all around him. He couldn't turn around, so he stood there, looking out over the frozen lake, wondering what would happen if it broke and he sank in. He carried the rock walking backward. Each step he took made the ice break more, fragments floated apart, bubbles gurgled beneath the thinned ice, and crack lines spidered all around like a huge white web slowly ensnaring him. Franklin remained calm as he felt the ice crackling and moving up and down. Five or six yards from the shore, the ice finally gave way and broke, and he fell into the slushy water—water so cold it would freeze him to the bone in seconds. But before he was completely swallowed up by the water, he threw the rock onto the shore and managed to crawl his way to firm ground. Blue in the lips and hands, and shivering, but smiling, he managed to chatter the words out, "I love you, Lynn."

Later, in December, Franklin flew home with Lynn to spend Christmas with her parents. Feeling nervous and awkward around her friends one night at a party, he got drunk and then drove crazily through the snow-packed streets, speeding through red lights and nearly killing them both. He left the next morning and she didn't return with him. Lynn had never seen this side of Franklin and the incident completely unnerved her.

She said she needed some time to think and that things between them were so intense, she wanted to slow down and get grounded. She called him later to tell him she was going to accept a job offer teaching English. He objected, arguing it would tear them apart, but she insisted it was only temporary. She needed to be around her friends, visit with her parents, and think about their relationship.

He drove around a lot during that period, revisiting the area where he had grown up. His thinking was getting worse and worse, and he now wondered if their time together was nothing more than a cheap affair. At one point she said that her friends would not understand. Understand what, he thought now, that he loved her, that he wanted a life with her?

He wrote to her, saying that he was ready to settle down, that he was prepared to spend his life with her. He didn't care what people thought or said; he promised her he would be true and they would have a good life. But her replies seemed cautious, mistrustful, and emotionally strained. He grew angry and accused her of playing him and his emotions—for her, he said, his love was all a game. This made her withdraw into silence and when he did hear from her again weeks later, she sounded relieved to have her life back to normal. She was back in her old apartment, having coffee with old friends before work and beers with girlfriends after work, and she was content to let their relationship cool off.

Over the next three months, they talked on the phone almost every night. He questioned her about why she was unprepared to commit herself to him and she in turn wondered how stable a life with him would be. She kept returning to the night when he got so drunk. It worried her. They went over the problems they had already encountered because of their age difference and cultural backgrounds. When Lynn asked him how he felt about marriage, again he backed away from saying he would marry her. He was afraid of not being able to measure up to her expectations and he said he wanted to first try living together. With some reservation, she agreed to jump-start their relationship again and flew down to Santa Fe for a weekend with him.

At his apartment, they talked long into the night, speaking truthfully and solemnly about their mutual fear of commitment, of failure, of hurting each other and being hurt. They couldn't articulate the contradiction that struck at the center of their souls: the desire to love and be loved, to give and yet take, to be together and alone, and last, the impulse to be courageous and fearful. Though they both admitted they had never loved anyone so intensely and deeply, perhaps the safest thing to do would be to give each other time and space, and if it was meant to be, they'd end up together. But as soon as they woke, they found that they couldn't stop crying and kissing and holding each other. They were quiet on the way to the airport and they wept as they parted.

Over the next two months they lived in separate worlds, dated other people, worked, and made new friends. They tried to forget each other but it was useless. Franklin called Lynn one day to tell her he had decided to move to Mexico. He left a message on her machine and she called him back that evening.

Lynn said she was due for a break from teaching and agreed to drive down to New Mexico and meet him at the hot springs.

He tried to sound nonchalant but his voice broke in places nevertheless.

Sunday morning he rose early, packed a lunch basket with various fruits, sandwiches, bottled water, and juice, and drove two hours to the hot springs. She looked as beautiful and stunning as she had that first day at the rodeo. It was a perfect day, blue sky, sunshine. At the springs a host of Chicano families was scattered around, and as Franklin and Lynn talked in one of the pools, they watched kids squeal with delight as they ran over the grassy meadows down into the stream to swim and splash. The scalding, mineral-green water made their flesh red and hot, and Franklin soon helped Lynn climb out of the muddy hole so they could rush down to the swiftly moving stream. They clambered precariously over river stones, hollered vigorously as they lay down in the freezing water, endured it for a few minutes, then leaped up and dashed back to the pool, where they sank down to their necks in the hot bubbling water.

They massaged each other, and then Franklin suggested that he hold her up while she floated in his hands. She stretched out, he put his palms under the small of her back for support, and she remained that way for a long time with her eyes closed. Then she did it to him, had him lean back and surrender to her hands under him. Everything but his eyes was underwater and he could hear the bubbles issuing from the earth below him, rising from the molten rock miles under the surface, making its way up thousands of feet to reach his body to caress him and ease him with its nurturing warmth. For a long time he drifted off with his eyes closed, feeling himself float away into particles that glided out into the universe, attaching to the spirit of all creatures and life-forms. Though neither could explain how, they both felt the power of the water that had flowed up from the center of the earth to bless them and unite them in a mystical resurgence of faith and hope.

"And that was it . . ." Franklin heard himself whisper, studying the photograph that captured their glazed looks in the hot sun. Early that day they'd been drinking tequila at the Tijuana Hotel, hours before the bullfights. The matadors stayed at the same hotel, and from time to time, one would sweep by on his way to a waiting car, or another would stand on a coffee table in the lobby with an attendant applying last-minute touch-ups to his costume.

Off in a corner beside windows that looked out over a patio garden, he and Lynn were drinking with a Chicano photographer wearing a bull's spine necklace and his boyfriend, the editor of an L.A. magazine. The two men had invited them over to join them in sampling exotic tequilas.

At around one in the afternoon, the four of them, feeling woozy, went out into the heat and headed down the winding cobblestone streets for the arena. The editor talked about how they had met, sharing that he had hired his lover to photograph the matadors. He looked at his companion and gave him a peck on the cheek, saying, "We are the perfect match!"

Lynn and Franklin lost the two men in the hordes of Mexicans streaming into the coliseum to watch the bullfights. They sat in the first rows, the ones closest to the pit, leaning their elbows on the railing wall so they could see the eyes and expressions of the bulls and matadors up close.

After all the time they had been together, Franklin knew how Lynn's eyes were sometimes the color of green summer sage but changed color depending on what kind of day it was or what clothes she was wearing. On rainy days they were dark green, on windy dry days they became the palest light blue, but on the day he first saw her they were the bluest blue he'd ever seen in his life. It was as if he were looking into the purest coastal waters surrounding an undiscovered island. On the day of the bullfights, they were red as the matador's cape.

Lynn was crying and getting angrier every time a new bull, heralded by the cries of spectators, proudly broke into the arena and the poised matador bravely faced the bull, lining up his sword under his cape in preparation for battle. After the bull had been stabbed, speared, and ignominiously dragged away, Lynn would rise and scream that it was wrong, that the bull didn't even have a chance. Her hysterics amused the Mexican crowd, who not only found her amusing but, judging by all the flirtatious stares, quite alluring.

Lynn changed her tune with the last bull. They had saved the bravest bull for the final fight, and a hushed awe rose from the spectators as the announcer stated that the bull was unrivaled,

the most valiant. Trumpets blared. The bull charged and immediately gored the matador in his thigh. With the matador pulled
off to the side so assistants could wrap his wound, the bull snorted
around the arena, daring anyone to challenge him. He trotted
around as if he were immortal, galloping wildly, swinging his
horns, and taunting the crowd to deliver him another victim. The
crowd loudly booed and ridiculed the matador, who now had
to save face and reappear for the showdown.

Lynn was the loudest, even the cruelest, standing and shouting for the bull to avenge the deaths of the other bulls. But then
the crowd grew quiet as the matador walked over to where
Franklin and Lynn sat, unleashed his sword from its scabbard,
pointed it at Lynn, and bowed. The crowd went berserk again,
tossing sombreros into the air, toasting their pulque cups and tequila bottles, while others bowed and waved. Souvenir-selling
kids rushed over and gave Lynn free roses, a mariachi trio ser-
enaded her with a song, and one young gentleman gave her a
beautiful Mexican cowboy hat, which she put on. One of the
Mexicans seated a few seats to Lynn's left leaned over and told
Lynn, "He will kill the bull in your honor! Because you are so
beautiful! He's paying homage to your beauty!" Lynn couldn't
hear what he said because of the noise from the crowd, nor could
she understand what this generous outpouring of affection meant,
but as she and Franklin looked around waving back in gratitude,
thousands of spectators smiled at them.

The crowd reeled in ecstatic hysteria as huge gates opened
up on the far side of the arena and men in uniforms brocaded

with glittering jewels came out on horseback with long spears and gradually formed a circle around the bull, surrounding him. The crowd fell deathly silent. Other novice matadors appeared with capes and smaller daggers. The circle tightened around the bull as the creature lunged with false starts in one direction and then another, trying to roll its massive eyes everywhere at once. Confused and alarmed, it charged at matadors wherever it saw them.

Although it could do nothing as daggers and swords plunged into its back and heart and chest, still it did not fall; it refused to go down. Blood drooling from its nose, gushing from its wounds, dribbling in red rivulets down its shimmering black hide, it charged again and again, only to be knifed and speared until the blood literally dripped in a curtain from its wounds and the bull turned red in the lowering sunlight. When it stood in one place, huffing, trying to breathe, pools of blood gathered under its belly. When it moved, scores of daggers planted deep in its muscles jiggled with its movements.

Crying and drinking more tequila, Lynn was yelling her heart out at the cowards when two men dressed in suits descended the bleachers. They escorted Franklin and Lynn up the concrete steps of the arena and around the top of it to the back, and then down into the area where the bulls were dragged after they were killed.

Franklin and Lynn felt disoriented as the two men positioned them under a rough-looking, open-air shed made of four telephone poles and a corrugated roof. Dizzied by too much tequila, the heat, and the roaring crowd, they held hands and waited. They remained as they were, until they heard the crowd give a concerted groan followed by a gasp, then a triumphant howl erupting in deafening celebration.

Seconds later, the big wooden arena doors swung open and a chariot of four horses, breathing foam from their nostrils, charged through dragging the dead bull behind them. Four other men—naked except for ragged and soiled shorts—appeared and unchained the bull that now rested on the ground under the shed.

The bull had not entirely expired and was still snorting out its last heaving breaths, when a giant of a man, wielding a medieval ax, and his cohort, a fierce ash-smudged midget with a sicklelike machete, grabbed Lynn and Franklin and stood them close to the bull.

Lying on its back, its big oval black-and-white eyes glaring and blood streaming from its nostrils and mouth, the bull bellowed mournful grunts as the midget bent down and ripped open the animal's torso from neck to groin. The giant next to him yanked the rib cage apart, and then the midget sank his hand into the bull's chest, held a cup next to a heart artery, and filled it with blood.

He withdrew his hand, turned, and, all spattered and smeared with blood and guts, handed the cup to Lynn, motioning for her to drink. Lynn looked at Franklin, who nodded, and she drank half of it, handing him the other half, which he drained. All the while, just beyond the shed, a mob of Mexicans, Americans, and Asians were shouting and waving fistfuls of money high above their heads, hollering for the testicles, horns, tongue, and penis. The midget stepped toward the crowd, swung his machete in an arc, and yelled that they better keep their distance. He then cut off a portion of the still warm and beating heart and handed it to Lynn. She bit off a part and chewed and swallowed it. Franklin did the same. They both understood there was no turning back; they had now committed to love and trust each other for life.

Runaway

....

The orphanage was to be doomed for demolition as soon as the nuns could arrange for suitable institutions or group homes to accept its more than four hundred boys. However, the children's relocation was not going as well as they had hoped, so the closure was still on hold—it would happen when it happened. Motorists passing along I-40 and pedestrians hurrying down Indian School Road would continue to see masses of boys rushing down from the second-story classrooms, shoving and jostling one another out the push-handle double doors of the ground floor. The boys would stream past the communal washrooms to the right, roughhouse their way west across the stony lot to the open-air big shed, and spread like a trembling earthquake over the playground. Massive telephone beams held up the corrugated roof of the big shed, which covered sixty or so picnic benches and tables. There the nuns shuffled cards and laid out hands of solitaire, and boys lounged on tabletops, talking, sleeping, or playing checkers and dominoes.

Ten years ago, when Runaway was first brought to the home at the age of six, he was out under the big shed on a summer morning when he saw a boy go into an epileptic attack. The boy squirmed and contorted on the concrete as nuns tried to pull his tongue out of his throat, and Runaway thought the school did that to kids—tortured them and forced them into madness. Runaway sat on a table under the big shed and cried and cried for days. Nobody could remember any boy who cried that long with such passionate effort. He used to believe that if he cried hard enough his parents might come and get him. No one ever told him his parents had been shot in an armed robbery and died from wounds later in the hospital. His aunt delivered him to the orphanage in the middle of the night, telling him that his mom and dad were off working far away and they'd come and get him when they were finished with their job. The nuns still remembered how Runaway sobbed from dawn to dusk for weeks and how he didn't stop until his grandma came to visit him. She was the only person in the world who loved him, and because he believed that, Runaway ran away so many times to be with her that his original name, Juanito, was used less and less by the nuns and the boys, and was eventually replaced with the name everyone knew him by—Runaway.

Every time after he ran away and was returned to the home, he would sit on a picnic table under the big shed with all his buddies surrounding him, and start his epic tale of adventure. "You should have seen her. My grandma's blind, but she's one bad old lady. If she could see, she would kick the shit out of those cops. She loves me. I'm in her trailer, a small little thing, hardly enough room for two, when we hear the cops outside. My grandma goes out, I'm holding her hand, and when we get outside, the cops say they're there to bring me back. She starts swinging her walking cane all around to keep the cops from getting me. I'm behind her while she's doing this, but they rush her, grab me, and

I'm carried away fighting these two goons, kicking and yelling, *'I'll be back. Grandma, I'll be back.'*"

Sometimes he went on with his beautiful lies until the church bell rang, signaling that afternoon playtime had ended. The boys would stream in from all directions on the field and playground to wash up before supper. After their evening meal, they would do their chores and watch TV for an hour in the playroom reserved for toddlers during the day. Around 7 P.M. they'd all be marched in twos to their respective dorms, where they'd put on their pajamas and then head for the bathroom. In front of a row of mirrors and sinks, the boys brushed their teeth, slicked their hair with daubs of greasy pomade, and preened themselves as if they were going out on dates.

One night, above the clamor, a kid masturbating in one of the toilet stalls groaned, "Ahh . . . ahhh."

"You squeezing your turkey, turkey . . ." a second kid's voice poked fun from another toilet stall.

"Ahhh . . . ahhh . . . ahhh."

"How many times you coming!"

"Ahhh . . ."

"Nobody comes that much!"

Despite the noisy turmoil, the sweetest rap floated angelically from a corner of the urinals: Runaway smacked a stick against the cast-iron lip of the urinal and harmonized with Kimo, a big Tongan boy, who slapped his stomach, shoulders, and buttocks, contributing some tribal conga sounds to the song, as Tesco and Osca, two Jamaican brothers, rapped.

"Stop this procrastination and get to bed!" scolded Sister Dolores, the dormitory nun. There was a sudden hush at the sinks and most of the boys scrambled out. Even the kid masturbating in the toilet stalls rushed out. But Sister Dolores's presence was lost on Runaway and his crew—the acoustics in the newly quiet washroom were great and they kept rapping.

Sister Dolores angrily rounded the wall separating the urinal from the sinks and stood there glaring.

"You," she said, her eyes drilling Runaway, "always the trouble!"

"We were just kicking it around before bed," Runaway said, out of breath and sweating, suffused with happiness from singing.

"You *kick it*," she hissed, "tomorrow morning, an hour before the others rise, to clean the side altars."

"Why? I haven't done anything," Runaway protested.

"You know the rules, it's bedtime, not rap time."

"It's always rap time," Tesco said.

"Got that," his brother Osca chimed in.

Sister Dolores frowned at them, then extended her arm toward the cots in the other room and commanded, "Bed!"

The next morning Runaway knelt at the communion railing, fervently praying at a small side altar to a wooden statue of the brown Virgen de Guadalupe, patron saint of the Chicanos.

"Help my grandma, she's alone, and needs you to do a miracle. Can you hear me?" He studied her brown lacquered eyes flickering with candle flames. The glimmering flames from the votive candles softened her expression and her gaze. "She's going blind, you know, and she can't hardly walk anymore."

The priest, Father O'Neil, startled Runaway. "You haven't started cleaning?"

Father O'Neil was a no-nonsense English priest with a weathered face, a red bulbous nose from too much Mass wine, and a sour disposition. Most of the boys knew about Father O'Neil's transgressive behavior with some of the kids, but it wasn't worth it to reproach him; the nuns would never believe it, and the unlucky kid who accused him would get a terrible beating. All they could do was warn newcomers to keep on their toes.

"I was about to—" Runaway started to say.

"Step on it."

Runaway picked up the feather duster and began dusting La Virgen again as Father recrossed the main altar toward his quarters.

"Do they listen?" Runaway called out to Father O'Neil.

Father O'Neil turned. "Who?"

Runaway pointed to the saints at the side altars.

"Start obeying the rules and they might."

He watched Father leave and then made a few disheartened swipes at La Virgen. He realized suddenly that she might not be able to hear him. He set down the feather duster and took her off the altar ledge. Emboldened by his act, he carried her to the pew and lay down with her. He unbuttoned his shirt and placed her next to his heart.

"Maybe," he whispered, "you couldn't hear my prayers. Now you can. They're even stronger in my heart."

He fell asleep praying, clutching her close against his naked chest. The last images he saw as he dozed off were the faces of other saints on the altars gazing at him lovingly.

The chapel darkened as the sun moved west across the sky. Bells sounded. Pigeons came in from the fields and landed on the ledge outside the stained glass window above the main altar. Nuns came and went without even noticing Runaway sleeping on the pew; they knelt at the communion railing, lit votive candles, and left. Then Father O'Neil entered with two altar boys.

"The choir will be singing Gregorian chants, and when they come to the verse—" He paused, noticing the feather duster on the floor. He picked it up and looked around. He found Runaway sleeping and when he saw the saint against the boy's bare chest, he slapped Runaway hard across the face, roaring, "How dare you! You heinous fiend!"

With his face burning and La Virgen violently yanked from his grasp, Runaway leaped up and dashed out of the chapel, confused about what was happening and what he had done to make Father so enraged.

He flew up the flight of stairs from the second floor to the third and crawled through the small door leading into the bell tower. A storm of pigeon feathers exploded in the air when he entered. The birds madly squeezed through the slats, cooing frantically. Runaway hugged his knees to his chest in a corner on the floor caked with feathers and bird droppings, shaking so badly that he welcomed the sudden deafening gong of the bells, which distanced him from his own fright and made the birds go even more crazy. After hours spent hiding in the bell tower, he finally came out and turned himself over to Sister Anna Louise.

She was the enforcer, a tall, broad-shouldered, grim-lipped German woman. She reminded Runaway of the picture in his history book of Napoleon. Often she'd surprise the kids with practice fire drills—when the alarm went off, all the kids would dive under their school desks. It was called the Sister Anna Louise drill, not because of the drill itself but because whenever she appeared on the playground, in hallways, or anywhere on the grounds, everyone dived for cover.

The next day she pulled Runaway out of class and escorted him to his dormitory. She had him pull down his pants and spanked him so many times that he lost count at thirty-eight, his butt so numb he couldn't feel the sting of the board anymore.

Dozens of boys played under the hot sun on the playground. Sitting on the sides of the sandbox, the older, rougher boys yelled, "Come try your luck! Hit 'em and win 'em. Try your luck!"

Boys crowded in and knelt at a line scratched in the dirt to shoot at the pyramids of marbles against the sandbox ten feet away. On all four sides, shooters jostled one another and marbles flew down the swept-dirt gallery, missing and banging hard against the metal. Other boys collecting the marbles got their knuckles smacked hard as their hands scurried in and out of the line of fire.

At the monkey bars, the risk takers did suicidal somersaults, some still with casts on their arms from breaking their limbs the last time. Unfazed, they threw crazy flips and crashed down onto the dirt on necks, backs, and knees. Younger boys were at the slides and teeter-totters, and near them, another group of boys played *piquete,* a Mexican top game. One player would throw his top into a circle drawn into the dirt, and the other players would try to crack his top in half with their tops before it stopped spinning. If the first player's top survived the bombing, then another player had to throw his top in and let the other boys try to bust that one. The dirt circle was always littered with splintered corpses.

Other kids sat along the ditch that ran around the playground, smoking cigarettes made of dried elm leaves and comic book paper; some walked the weed and dirt field, others raced go-carts on the asphalt court. The go-carts were made of pieces of rotting wood and baling wire, with rusty bicycle-rim steering wheels and wobbly, rubberless wagon wheels. Some played basketball on the other half of the court, a black square marked with a coal rock indicating where the backboard, rim, and net used to be.

Runaway and his crew stood in the right field, rapping and harmonizing while waiting for Marcello, the midget coach, to hit them a pop-up. Runaway told them the next ball would be his—he was going to catch it. Meanwhile he sang backup lyrics, Kimo slapped his body with his glove, and Tesco and Osca ricocheted rap lyrics.

Runaway shuffled back and forth kicking listlessly at the dirt, singing, swatting his glove against his leg, and turning around in the outfield wishing a pop-up would come his way. He rapped hard and fast, then squinted at Coach Marcello at home plate, in his boots and cowboy hat, swinging the bat in front of the galvanized-pipe and chicken-wire backstop. Coach Marcello looked around, gave Runaway a vague gesture with his head as though he intended to hit the ball to him, then threw up the ball and smacked it. Runaway, singing and harmonizing with Tesco and Osca, spread his legs apart, leaned forward, and slapped his glove, ready to catch it.

The ball arched over the infield but sailed left, to Clubfoot Tony. Runaway watched him quickly hop forward a few times to gain momentum before he threw the ball to second base. Big Noodle scooped it up and fired it to home plate. Again coach Marcello looked at Runaway as if he were going to hit him one. It could be that right-handed midget coaches couldn't hit to right field, thought Runaway, as he smacked the inside of his glove. He liked hearing the pop it made when he punched the leather so he whacked the glove again, keeping beat with another rap song. He leaned forward on the balls of his feet to show Marcello he was ready and to urge him to hit a grounder, all the while singing to the rhythm of the song.

Marcello hit a waist-high line drive to shortstop. Intending to cry out "It's all yours" or "You got it baby," Runaway instead yelled, "Runaway!" This word meant a kid had gone over the fence; it was like calling out, "Escape!" Maybe out of frustration at waiting so long for a ball, or from an unconscious yearning to see his grandma again, or simply from an urge to run away himself, he had shouted it. The kids around the baseball diamond glanced at Runaway, unsure why he had cried out the alarm.

Tesco and Osca stopped rapping and asked Runaway, "Who ran?" He didn't answer so they grinned and followed suit, yelling, "Runaway!" All three recognized the opportunity for an unplanned excursion through the free lands beyond the orphanage boundary lines.

Kimo, realizing it was a hoax, screamed loud, "Runaway!," hoping to incite the boys to dash for the ditch and over the fence to chase the supposed fugitive who had fled the premises unseen.

"Don't let him get away," Marcello cried from the backstop as the boys broke for the fence line.

Peanut Head, the shortstop, had taken his eyes off the ball, and it had grazed the upper part of his glove, bounced up, and hit him in the cheek. Peanut Head gave a pained look, shook off his glove, and knelt down on one knee holding his head. But even in pain, he quickly recovered, roused by cries from other kids: "Runaway! Runaway!"

Marcello looked around in distress at the boys dropping their gloves and stampeding toward freedom. "Catch him! Bring him back to me," he exhorted as he watched the stream of boys jumping and trampling the fence. The hesitant boys, as though first making sure it was okay with Marcello, searched the fence line with puzzled expressions on their faces before rushing headlong behind the others, over the fence, and into Mr. Scrip's orchard. Scrip was a crabby alcoholic farmer who blasted buckshot at kids he caught stealing watermelons from his fields.

Runaway's mind drifted aimlessly as he sprinted, leaping over tumbleweeds, ducking under tree limbs, snapping an apple off a branch, and eating it as he raced on. He caught up to the kids in front of him, passing Clubfoot Tony and tossing the apple core to Flood, the fastest kid in school.

"Yeah, who ran?" asked Cuckoo Clock, running up beside him.

"Who knows," Runaway replied, smiling at his own secret.

They charged past the orchards and headed west across the open fields and past the KQEO radio towers with the red blinking lights—the same lights Runaway stared at through his dorm window before going to sleep each night.

When they reached town they crossed the busy boulevard, Rio Grande, purposely slowing down enough to make the cars stop for them. They jammed into Wells Market and minutes later were chased out by Mr. Perez.

"You don't have money, don't come in! Little thieves. Offspring of dogs," Mr. Perez said, swatting them back through the door with his white apron.

The boys laughed it off, their pockets already stuffed with candy and their mouths frothing with the bittersweet fizzies they had stolen.

Kimo came out with a big bag of candy and soda pop and sat down on the street curb. He handed out portions to Tesco, Osca, and Runaway. They quickly finished the sweets and then stood up to leave. Runaway lingered on the sidewalk.

"Come on," Tesco said.

There was a familiar expression on Runaway's face.

Hoping to dissuade his pal from running and getting into trouble again, Tesco said, "We need to practice our new songs and we can't without you."

Osca said, "Ah, man, there ain't no runaway."

"There is now," Runaway said, his tone defiant.

Kimo warned, "Homeboy, they're going to beat you bad—"

"I have to see if she's okay," Runaway said, staring to the south where his grandma lived. He threw his soda bottle into the weeds and nodded to his crew; as he started to jog, they commenced singing a rap song he had written. He turned when he heard them, waved, and then scrambled over a wall. He took off behind the store, climbed over a cinderblock fence, and disappeared.

After a while, he fell into a runner's trance, crossing fields, going along ditch banks through different barrios and ghettos, passing foul-smelling industrial yards, sneaking across municipal building parking lots, and cutting around city parks until he found himself on the outskirts of the city. He reminisced about his most recent visit with his grandmother, which bore no resemblance to the imaginative version he had described to his friends.

★   ★   ★

The journey from the orphanage to his grandma's trailer was long and exhausting and took all day. He knew that he would arrive tired and hungry, but happy. His grandma would give him a big hug, and after having him get the cookies and milk, she'd sit him down next to her on the tattered couch and they'd flip through the old family photo album, with Runaway narrating as he had during his last visit.

"In this one a man has suspenders on. He wears his pants high and shoves his cuffs into his boots . . ."

"That was your uncle Louis. He was a sweet man." Her stubby fingers went to the next photo, some of them so old they had serrated edges and were faded completely in places.

She lifted her head and stared up blindly, recalling from memory which photo she had her finger on, and saying, "Ah, yes, this must be your uncle Max. Where is this photo? In front of a barn . . ."

"Yes!" Runaway exclaimed. "How do you do that, Grandma?"

"Oh, there's more than one way to see things. I have them etched in my mind." Runaway was impressed as she recounted the history of the photos he looked at.

"Here is your uncle Tomas who died in World War II," she recounted. And, "Your aunt Valentina—she was so beautiful, she had such a promising future. She went into the world with the brightest hopes and all of it ended with her living along interstates in squalid trailer parks with men who drank and abused her."

When she came to a photo of one of her own seven children, she wondered aloud why they had turned on her. She began to weep and she told Runaway how her kids had signed a paper saying she was incompetent to run her ranch and how, with the help of attorneys, they had been appointed executors of her estate. A short time later, sight unseen, they had some quack doctor diagnose her as mentally ill, and afterwards her kids sold the land, split up the cash, and bought themselves houses in the city. She looked down at Runaway with large brown eyes clouded with cataracts and asked, "How could my own kids label their mother mad, steal my land, put me in this old trailer on a dirt lot?"

Runaway couldn't answer her, and he carried a big grudge against his aunts and uncles. There wasn't a thing wrong with his grandma except she was fat. Her blindness didn't slow her down. After sitting on the couch a bit, she'd have to grab her cane in one hand, place her other hand on Runaway's shoulder, and push herself up.

"Help me, sweet dove," she would say.

One time, he helped lift her as she leaned on him and walked the few steps to the toilet. She was so large she couldn't fit her whole body in the toilet cubicle, so she sat on the toilet with one leg and arm sticking out into the small hallway.

"I'm so sorry, my prairie dove, so sorry," she said.

And Runaway could see why she was sorry. While laboring to get to the toilet, she had peed down her leg. Pinching his nostrils so he wouldn't gag, he told her, "It's okay, Grandma," and knelt down to wipe the floor clean.

He cut across fields now, and it was cold enough that he could see his breath in the darkness against the moonlight. He sensed that his grandma needed him. He didn't know the names of the paved streets or dirt roads that led to her house, but he could find the way. Like a bird that knows its nest is over there, Runaway knew, so he climbed over fences and stumbled down streets, heading to his grandma's.

Shivering, he crossed a wide parking lot and saw a nondescript, whitewashed brick building where second-hand clothes and used items, really used, were sold. He looked through the plate glass window and noticed that most of the stuff had to be fourth- and fifth-time hand-me-downs—on their last stop before the trash bin. Blowing on the glass and cleaning it with a hand, he caught sight of a stack of sweaters in a cardboard box. He went around the building, found a wrought-iron ladder that ran to the roof, and climbed it. Pushing aside the swamp cooler, he slid his legs down into the duct hole, kicked out the air vent grill, and leaped down into the store.

At first he thought they might be real, but then he realized he was standing before two armless mannequins. He touched the plaster boobs, and then, spooked by their real-looking eyes, he turned them around and signed a cross over himself. Slipping out of his shoes, socks, shirt, and pants, he picked out a "new" outfit. He cuffed the pants and shirtsleeves, stuffed newspapers into a pair of Stacy Adams shoes, and looped a belt twice around his waist to hold his dress pants up. When Grandma felt the fine material he was wearing, he'd be like those men in the stories she told him, the men she had dated when she was young and voluptuous, working in a New Orleans river bar, one of the girls wearing a bunny costume, perched on a swing above the heads of the patrons who pushed her back and forth as she sang.

Grabbing a paper bag with plastic handles, he started filling it with everything he could—big panties, voluminous bras, a couple pairs of black stockings, a fake pearl necklace, and two colored-bead wristbands. In another corner he found velvet paintings of Elvis and another of a bull charging at a bullfighter's red cape. Setting the bag down, he silently imitated Elvis, singing into an invisible microphone in his fist, and then, using a huge pair of panties as a cape, he taunted an imaginary bull charging at him. In the midst of one of his whirls, his eye caught the glimmering cash register.

The drawer was open and the change bins were brimming with pennies. He immediately filled his front and back pockets, which bulged and sagged so badly he had to retighten his belt. He was still adjusting his pants when headlights suddenly raked across the dark interior of the store. He ducked.

Peeking out the window, he saw a cop car pulling in. He bolted for the vent, leaped up, grabbed the edge, swung his feet up, and hung upside down like a monkey from a tree branch. Just then the cops entered and swung their flashlights around.

"I don't see anything," the Indian cop said.

"We'll come by in the morning and tell Mr. Chavez to put in an alarm. Third time this month someone's called about prowlers here," the Chicano cop said.

They were leaving when they heard a sound. It grew louder. They turned, aimed their light beams at the sound on the floor, and saw pennies sprinkling down. Their light beams went up and followed the rain of pennies to Runaway, hanging upside down from the vent.

"I'll be damned."

"Runaway . . . we're getting tired of you," the cop complained and shook his head.

They took Runaway to a holding facility for juveniles, where he slept on a concrete bench in a cell; a policeman would drive him back to the orphanage at dawn. They didn't say much, having been through this several times; it was becoming a routine.

The police cruiser drove under the St. Anthony's Boy's Home arch that spanned the entrance, supported by granite columns on each end. The policeman followed the circular gravel driveway and stopped at the entrance to the main building, where two nuns stood in immaculate white smocks.

Runaway stared gloomily out the backseat window and marveled at the blooming rose bushes bundled against the base of the building. He gazed left at the grass encircled by the drive-way. It was mowed and trimmed, and dew sparkled from the green blades in the bright sunlight. Sparrows chirped and shook their wings on window ledges. At the bell tower pigeons flut-tered around, squeezing and squirming in and out of the slats.

Having rolled down his window to smell the grass and roses, he heard the familiar hum of voices churning in the air from the playground and he yearned for the company of his friends. The image of his grandma in his mind, of her all alone in that small trailer, made him angry. He didn't care how they punished him; the effort to see his grandma was worth it.

The policeman was greeted by Sister Superior Pauline and Sister Anna Louise. They spoke with furtive expressions on their faces, glancing at him with conspiratorial concern. Runaway tried in vain to read their lips. His mouth and throat were dry and he swallowed hard. All he heard the policeman say when he took him out of the car was, "You're going to have to do something about this, Sisters." Runaway could see the nuns' discomfort as they sheepishly apologized to the officer.

Sister Superior Pauline, head of the nuns, hardly meddled in the boys' affairs. She was nice but busy, and was always either in her office meeting officials or attending civic events. Short and stout with a kind, oval face, she looked at him with empathy, unlike Sister Anna Louise, whose eyes gleamed darkly and sig-naled his impending punishment.

Something inside Sister Anna Louise had turned malignant, and whatever it was fixed its bitter blade-edged glare on him.

Her eyes held his and told him he was in for a severe spanking. Runaway wondered which paddle she would use—they were lined up on the wall in room number 5. That was the room that instilled terror in every boy, and Runaway had made it his second home. She would probably use the big tennis racket paddle, twelve inches across, two and a half feet long. Put her weight into it too, because his running away and her order for him to stop opposed each other like fierce face-to-face combatants, neither taking a step back. As his runaways became more frequent, her spankings only became more brutal.

About three months ago she had beat him so badly, for so long, that when he showered a few days later, he saw that his back, legs, and buttocks were black. He had gone out to the playground, searched everywhere for Flood, who was one of the few black kids in the orphanage, found him, and said, "Hey, I'm going to be black like you."

Flood didn't know what he meant.

"Look, I'm going to be black," Runaway repeated. He drew up his shirt and turned around so Flood could view his back—bruised black, purple, and pale yellow.

"Man, you can't be black by getting beat black, you gotta be born black."

It had greatly disillusioned Runaway, because he was tired of being himself and having his same old life everyday. He fully believed that a deserving person could be transformed, if the divine powers willed it so. He secretly supposed that all one had to do was gain the favor of the angels and it would happen.

He kept hoping to wake up one day as a butterfly, one of those big yellow monarchs, or as a grasshopper, a horny toad, or even one of the pigeons perched outside the stained glass window with white wings and black feathers running down the middle of its breast.

After past runaways, what really hurt him was losing privileges. On Friday nights, when he had to scrub classroom floors, the rest of the boys would be in the auditorium playing murder in the dark. The boys were split up into two sides at opposite ends of the auditorium and a balled up sock was placed on the floor between them. The object of the game was to bring the sock back to your side. When the lights were turned off, both sides moved toward the sock. Anyone caught moving when the lights came back on was out of the game. In the dark you could get another kid in a headlock and be ready to slam him to the floor, but when the lights came on, you had to freeze your position. And when the lights went out, you resumed your crazed destruction. The timing of the lights going on and off was random—sometimes they stayed off a long time and other times flicked on and off quickly, weeding out the players. Runaway missed punching, kicking, and wrestling with his friends.

Sister Superior Pauline went up to her office, and after she left Sister Anna Louise, said, "Well, you've shamed us again, haven't you." Instead of to room number 5, she escorted Runaway to his dorm, saying on the way there, "Understand, young man, your grandmother is blind, she has health problems, and all you do is worry her."

"You don't have to be able to see to love someone," Runaway said.

She slapped him, then pulled his ear, and lengthened her stride. "I'll teach you to talk back!"

In the dorm, she pulled a paddle from under her smock, had him lean over with his pants down, and delivered fifty smacks to his bare butt.

The next day, Runaway was buffing the tiles in the chapel. The industrial buffer was twice his weight and he had trouble controlling it as it swung back and forth in wide arcs. Runaway turned off the buffer when he saw his crew stealthily creep in.

Kimo, Tesco, and Osca smiled at him. Kimo held up a bottle of wine and then started swaying his hips and rapping impromptu. "No time to hear cheap talk, we got the priest's best wine, prayers and blessings may be fine, but wine from his private stock we'll take anytime."

"We had to sneak out of the kitchen to see how you are," Osca said.

The three resumed the song, singing with eyelids shut tight, thinking of on-the-spot lyrics, and wailing out their versions of R & B and hip-hop rhymes, which echoed in the cavernous chapel. Kimo slapped his thighs and stomach, and Osca and Tesco blended in their tunes, while Runaway, using a finger as a baton, kept their spontaneous jam session together. They settled down, huddling on their haunches in a corner hidden by the pews. They sipped and passed the bottle around.

Runaway hummed the song back. "That's bad . . . awesome shit," he said.

Osca gave the bottle to Runaway. "Glad to have you back, homeboy."

Kimo asked, "They paddle you bad?"

Tesco said, "No such thing as a good paddle."

Runaway stood, lifted his shirt, and pulled down his pants. "I'm black all over." He smiled, and they laughed when he told them about his old belief that he'd turned black. "I really believed I was changing." He paused. "Didn't you ever want to change? I mean, don't you get tired of being you?"

"Damn you stupid!" Osca exclaimed.

"Wouldn't it be cool though if you could change into five things—say a black person today, a white person tomorrow, a bird, a woman—" Runaway said.

"I'd be back on my island, a volcano man, erupting and roaring all this lava out," Kimo said.

"I'd be a big joint in a pretty woman's mouth," said Tesco.

"I'd be something else in a pretty woman's mouth," Osca said.

"You guys shouldn't be talking that way in a chapel," Runaway said.

"Just the buzz," Kimo said, smiling.

A dull noise came from the confessional. Kimo capped the wine, stuffed the bottle into his waistband, and left with the rest.

Runaway went back to buffing. No more than a minute later, Father O'Neil came out of the confessional, red-faced. He gave Runaway a frown, and went through the doorway to his quarters. After waiting a sufficient time, Runaway turned off the buffer and went to the confessional. He slowly opened the door and saw an Indian boy, about twelve years old, cringing in terror in the corner on the floor. Runaway reached out to him but the kid recoiled.

"Yeah, you okay, I'm not going to hurt you. Let's go to the nurse—she's cool. Come on, let's go. We don't want him coming back."

The boy didn't move.

Clutching his arm, Runaway pulled him out of the confessional, and led him out of the chapel and down the stairwell and along the hallway to the infirmary. There he walked right up to Sister Theo, the infirmary nurse, dressed in her white linen smock. A giant sweet-faced German nun, Sister Theo liked Runaway and he was fond of her because she was nice and reminded him of his grandma. She sat the Indian boy on one of the three tube-iron cots and questioned him at length, but he didn't respond. The other two cots had boys in them with broken arms. They all stared as Sister Theo shined a pen flashlight into the Indian boy's eyes.

"He's not responding," she said, turning off the light. "Where did you find him?"

Runaway knew that if he told the truth he'd incur the wrath of Father O'Neil.

"He was on the steps. I think he's a new boy. Maybe Father O'Neil tried to confess him. You know what he says, all us kids are possessed, maybe a devil's in him too, that's what he says about me."

"Don't ever believe that. You have God's good love in you and so does this boy. I think Father O'Neil watches too much TV."

"Wish I could watch TV, I miss the *Simpsons,*" Runaway said. "I'm still being punished."

He followed her up the two tiny steps into the pharmacy dispensary, no larger than a long narrow closet, with glass cabinets stocked with medicine bottles along the wall.

"He won't even let me touch him," Sister Theo said, concerned. "He flinches, and that's not a good sign. We should call Sister Anna Louise."

"I'll take him to the playground, he'll be okay. Remember what you say, play is the best medicine for a boy."

She wasn't sure though. She studied the Indian boy again and said, "If I keep him here, Sister Anna Louise will inevitably show up and accuse me of coddling him." She looked briefly lost in thought, and then said, "Well, at the slightest trouble, you bring him back to me."

Sister Theo grabbed some candy from a jar and returned to the boy. She handed a piece to him but he didn't even acknowledge her presence. "Do you want to talk?" she asked. The boy gave no response.

Runaway broke in, "You know what, I have a scratched knee, Sister Theo. My elbow and ankle hurt . . ." Sister Theo reached into her apron pocket and stuffed a handful of yellow lemon drops into his jeans.

"You ran again. You know you shouldn't," she said and patted his back. She motioned to the Indian boy to stay put for a minute and led Runaway out back, past the screen door, into her small garden bursting with every fragrance in the world.

The garden was enclosed by a transparent plastic tarp tent that she rolled up during spring and summer. She pointed out various plants. "That one cures earaches and this one tooth-aches. For a stomachache boil this leaf. And you know what this one does? It's a rose and it's been known to cure a broken heart."

"Wish there was one for blindness."

Sister Theo snipped a rosebud with her fingernails and placed it in Runaway's shirt pocket. "Put this on the side altar at Saint Anthony's feet—he'll send your love to your grandma."

"Do you have anything for arthritis?"

"Not a cure but something to alleviate the pain." She looked at her own hands. "When it gets real bad, I pray. Put these petals at the side altar with Saint Francis and pray that he lessen the pain of your grandma's arthritis." They sat on the bench in the gar-den and quietly looked around at all the different flowers.

"How about plants for luck?"

"The four-leaf clover, you find them in the grass."

She looked through the screen door to check on her pa-tient. "Oh my," she gasped, "he's gone."

"Don't worry, Sister, I'll find him. He probably went to the playground. And he'll get over his fright, I've seen lots of boys like that when they first come here."

★   ★   ★

A week later in class, Runaway accompanied Sister Rita as she sang a Latin hymn. He stood beside her in front of the blackboard and sang as melodiously as he could. Runaway was infatuated with Sister Rita—a tall, olive-skinned Arab nun with long sensuous hands and full lips. She was in her dark habit, a white collar framing her cinnamon face, a dark mole on her left cheek and long eyelashes. He stared at the flecks of spittle at the corner of her mouth, at her thick red tongue as her lips opened to sing the Gregorian Latin mass lyrics. When she finished, she placed her hand on Runaway's shoulder, and he immediately clutched it.

"Very good," Sister Rita said, beaming down on Runaway, her teeth white and straight as new shiny pearls. Runaway was ingratiating, even shy, as he averted his eyes and stared at the veins on her brown hand. Kimo raised his hand.

"Yes, Kimo," Sister Rita said.

"We'd like to rap, I mean we made up a tune for you," he said.

"No, Sister," Runaway said, afraid they were up to something, "there's no time to rap, we have to practice for the choir."

Kimo looked at Runaway and with a teasing tone in his voice said, "Just a little song we wrote for Sister Rita."

Tesco grinned. "It'll help us get ready for the choir."

"Exemplary Christians . . ." Kimo said.

They all looked over at Kimo with his big words as if he were a total dumb-ass.

Osca said, "That don't even sound English, mon . . ."

Osca led off with rhyming innuendos about Runaway's love for Sister Rita. She didn't understand his Jamaican slang, but it was explicit enough to leave Runaway red-faced. Ever resilient, Runaway slapped Sister Rita's desktop with a nice drumbeat, and Kimo fell in behind him with body-slap beats, as Runaway whipped his head and hips back and forth, conducting the crew on a hot-lick kick.

Just as they had finished, Sister Anna Louise entered. She whispered something to Sister Rita and pointed to Runaway. Sister Rita nodded to him and Sister Anna Louise escorted him out of the room.

They walked out of the main building, toward the communal washroom. "We've spanked you so many times you've worn the paddles thin," Sister Anna Louise said. "You've buffed the chapel floors to mirrors. We're going to try something else, a new project—to wash all the windows on the building, but first, there's something else you have to do." She swung open the door to the washroom.

Runaway grimaced at the biting odor of antiseptic detergents. The cement floor, lockers, cylindrical shower bays, and huge concrete tubs for washing hands and feet were cleaned spotless. Straight ahead of them, on a bench, was the Indian boy he'd helped a week earlier. Except this time he was caked in grime and it made Runaway freeze in his tracks. He'd never seen a boy so dirty.

"You're to clean and change him. Here's his change of clothes and a towel, washcloth, and soap. He doesn't speak. He was here for a week and ran away, the police found him roaming the prairie. Get to it now . . ." She pinched her nose and winced at the stink, then shook her head and left.

In the silence Runaway listened to the showers drip, trying not to gag at the wild stench filling the room. The boy's waist-length, tangled black hair was matted with dirt, twigs, and bits of stickers. His neck and arms had scratches and blood smears; he had scabs on his knuckles. He wore a torn plaid shirt and ripped jeans and old shoes that were rotten and cracked. The boy's face was hollow and vacant, and he stared down unblinking, as if Runaway wasn't even there.

Runaway walked around the shower bays, listening to the dripping sound and the scraping of his shoe soles. He didn't know what to do; he had never been asked to make a boy wash himself. Every time he came out from behind a shower, he shot a glance at the boy to see if he was looking, but the boy hung his head in brooding stillness. Runaway stopped by the concrete foot tubs. The outer rim was wide enough to sit on, and he jumped up onto it, sat with his legs dangling, and looked at the kid.

He swung around, pressed the stainless steel lever at the tub's base, and from the dozen or so nozzles sticking out of the concrete tub stem, an umbrella of water sprayed out. He looked behind him to see if the boy saw it, but the boy's head was still downturned. He thought maybe he should show the boy again that the water wasn't going to harm him. Runaway took off his shoes and socks, rolled up his pant legs, and with his bare foot pressed down the lever again. He rinsed his feet, cupped his hands under the water, and splashed his face.

"Yeah, you scared?" Runaway asked, sitting on the bench next to the kid, drying off with the towel and putting his socks and shoes back on. "You stink!" he said. He paced the area between the bench and tubs. "There's nothing to be afraid of," he said. He checked his pockets. "Here." He placed three shiny new pennies on the bench. "If Sister Anna Louise comes back and finds you're not cleaned, guess who's getting an ass whipping? Not you . . ."

They sat on the bench in silence and stared at the floor. Runaway had never met a boy with so little emotion, so lost in his own world. He wondered what had happened to him and how he could get him to talk about it. Maybe if he bribed him with marbles or chocolates he would wash up.

"I'll tell you about being afraid. See, the cops were chasing my friend and me. It was close to dark but you could still see. We were running back to my grandma's, and we came to this ditch filled with water. My friend jumped in and swam against the current and made it to the other side. He kept yelling for me to jump, but I was afraid. Finally, with the cops close behind, I was still afraid but I had no choice but to jump. I got to the other side and as I got up, a hand grabbed me from under the water, trying to pull me down and drown me. My friend tightened both his hands around my right hand and pulled as hard as he could, but the hand under the water was pulling me down. It was stronger. Every time

my friend pulled me up, it pulled me down harder. I started claw-
ing at the dirt banks to get out, yelling for help. Water was filling
my mouth, I couldn't breathe. When my friend screamed out it
was La Llorona, I really got scared—she's the witch that roams the
ditches at night looking for bad kids to drown. And I knew it was
her, I could feel her sharp nails in my skin, look—" He pulled up
his pant leg and stuck his shin under the kid's face to show him
the white scars just above his ankle bones. He continued, "She
was scratching and tugging hard to drown me. My friend knew it
too, he pulled even harder, almost tearing my arm out, and I was
kicking at her until we finally broke her grip. He pulled me up,
and I took off running faster than I ever had. My pant legs were
torn, my ankles bleeding, I even lost my shoe. I wanted to get it
back so I returned to the ditch the next day. I took some friends
and we all had rocks in our pockets and a bunch in our hands. We
were going to kill La Llorona, so she couldn't drown any more
kids. We got to the ditch and closed the gate off until the water
drained down to the bottom in that part. Guess what? Right where
La Llorona had me there was a mattress spring. A piece of my pants
was still stuck in the wire coil and my shoe was hooked to a sharp
wire that was sticking up. Every time I get scared now, I think
about that mattress spring. That's what fear is, a mattress spring."

The boy gave no indication that he'd even heard the story.
Same gloomy expression, same haunting shadows in his face, same
enveloping solitude.

Runaway got up, walked around the curtained bays with six
shower stations apiece, completed the loop, approached the boy,

looked at him for a long time, turned around, and went out of the washroom. He stood outside the door, bright sunshine blinding him momentarily, as kids' excited voices called him from the playground to join them. He breathed in, then out, and went back in.

Inside, water dripped loud and hard from showerheads onto the tin stall floors. The door behind him threw a slice of light slowly from left to right, illuminating the kid, who still sat with head down, body immobile.

Runaway wrapped the towel around his face like a veil, and carefully, with two fingers, he unbuttoned the boy's shirt. There were fresh welts on the boy's back, and Runaway felt a surge of anger toward the person responsible for them. He took off the boy's shoes and pants and saw his legs had sores on them. Runaway clenched his teeth, forcing himself to get it over with, do what he had to do. He closed his eyes as the boy's underpants dropped and he stood naked. Then he opened them and gently pushed the boy toward a shower stall.

He turned the water on, adjusted the handle to lukewarm, and moved the kid into the stall, under the nozzle. He had so much dirt on him that water ran brown off his skinny body. Runaway took the soap and washcloth and placed it in the boy's hand but they slipped right out, without the boy making even the slightest effort to clutch them.

Runaway, at the end of his patience, pissed off and self-conscious, grabbed the soap and washcloth and pushed the boy a little to show him he didn't like doing this, and soaped him up roughly. As he rinsed the suds off the boy's arms and back, he noticed red liquid mixing with the brown water in the drain. He followed the red liquid up the boy's legs to the buttocks and realized where the blood was coming from. He was incapable of moving for some minutes, watching the rivulets of blood pulse down the kid's legs, swirling into the water.

Now, with an entirely different attitude, not caring about the water wetting his own arms and face and spattering his shirt and pants, he washed the boy's body gently, almost caressing his arms with the cloth, raking his fingers through the boy's black hair, combing it down with his fingers, patting the cloth and soap over the welts, aiming the nozzle at the boy's arms, legs, and stomach, rinsing the soap off his body from his head to his toes, his hands soothing and reassuring the boy that it was all right.

He led him out and dried him off, careful not to rub the welts too hard; he swiped the towel behind his ears, under his chin, under his arms and stomach, and down his legs to his feet. He combed out the boy's hair with his fingers and braided it into a simple pony-tail. He dressed him and didn't feel embarrassed like he thought he would. Then he washed the boy's shoes in the tub, wiped them as dry as he could, and slipped them on him. All finished, he stepped back and appraised his work, beaming with satisfaction.

Runaway opened the door and they walked into the afternoon's bright sunlight. "I don't know what your name is, so until you tell me, I'll just call you 'Yeah.' You call me Runaway. You hang with me, no one's going to hurt you."

★ ★ ★

He went to meet his crew at the coal pile behind the incinerator. He sat the Indian boy against the wall of the toilet building outside and then he walked over to his friends.

They were arguing about something.

"No—no—," Tesco was saying, "we got to get serious, quit fooling around, we're back-stepping—remember our lyrics."

Osca said, "I'm back-stepping? I'll be on your ass, brother, like grease on a ham bone. Anything we chop is better than what's on MTV."

Runaway turned around to check on Yeah, who was still on the concrete slab, and raised his hands to interrupt them. "I want to bring him in," Runaway said.

Everybody got quiet and Kimo said, "You mean put him under our wing or let him join the crew."

Osca asked, "Don't he have any friends?"

"He's new," Runaway said, "and he's crazy—don't talk—don't do anything."

"Crazy qualifies him to be with us," Kimo said.

The Indian boy wasn't paying attention to their conversation. He sat against the bathroom brick wall, shaking something in one hand and tapping a rock against the concrete with his other.

Kimo said, "We can put him in to keep beat."

"Good idea. And I asked Sister Rita," Runaway said, "if we could perform at the Christmas party next week. There's supposed to be some sorority club coming from the university. We have to practice, but first let's go over and talk to him."

Yeah didn't look up at them; instead, staring into his palm and slowly opening it, he revealed two large-caliber bullets. The crew stopped, wondering nervously what he was up to. He placed one bullet on the concrete and pointed it toward the chapel building. He took the rock and slammed it down on the back end of the bullet, and a loud roar sent the crew diving for cover behind the coal pile.

Still huddled there, they all peeked out at Yeah, and slowly Runaway came around and said, "Drive-by, Indian style."

Tesco said, "Definitely qualifies as crazy."

One by one they rose and approached the Indian boy, who was placing the other bullet down.

"Whoa, that's another attention grabber . . ." Kimo said. "Yo Bullet Boy, don't point that cap this way."

Yeah smacked it but it was a dud.

"You tap a mean rock. You's good," Osca said. "But Yeah ain't no name, we're gonna call you 'Bullet.'"

"I like that," Runaway said, and looked at the Indian boy. "What do you think—Bullet sound okay?"

The Indian boy smiled faintly.

"He's been through a lot—treat him straight up," Runaway said. The crew grouped around Bullet and they headed for the playground.

It was a week before Christmas and the crew was in the auditorium getting ready to practice their rap songs for the play.

Bunches of decorations hung over the stage, red and green shiny bunting swooped everywhere, a Christmas tree was fully decorated, and all the radiators around the auditorium had glitter flakes on them. It was a festive time; the crew was sitting on the stage waiting.

"I want to try this new song out about Cesar Chavez," Runaway said.

"Write one next about Marley," Tesco said.

"Got it," Runaway said.

"Can't start without Osca. Sister Rita, where's he at?"

"Sister Anna Louise took him to Sister Superior's office," Sister Rita said.

Runaway grabbed a branch of mistletoe and lofted it above his head. "Sister Rita, where do I put this?"

Kimo said, "You better stop that."

Sister Rita came over and gave Runaway a peck on the cheek. "It's Christmas," she said, "and you can hang it over the exit door."

Osca finally walked through the entrance at the far end of the auditorium. They yelled and waved him on but Osca's steps were tentative and he looked troubled. He approached the stage, and his brother Tesco sat on the edge. Runaway, Kimo, and Bullet crouched down behind Tesco.

"They want to split us up, Tes, send me to Boys' Town," Osca said.

Tesco said, "That ain't going to happen, little brother. Only place we going back to is the island—together."

That night, Runaway lay on his bunk in the dormitory, looking at the ceiling while Bullet, in the next bunk, polished his brogans. The rest of the crew was directly across the aisle harmonizing in low tones so Sister Dolores wouldn't come out of her sleeping quarters at the head of the dorm.

Runaway asked Bullet, "You got anybody coming to see you on Christmas?"

Bullet shook his head no.

"How about you guys—Tesco, Kimo, Osca, you got anybody?"

They all shook their heads.

"I hate holidays, especially Christmas," Runaway said.

Boys were coming from the bathroom, putting away their toothbrushes, getting under the sheets, kneeling by their bunks and praying. At the head of the dorm Sister Dolores appeared. "Lights off in five minutes," she said, and went back into her room.

About thirty minutes after the lights were off, when most of the boys were snoring or on the verge of falling asleep, Runaway said to the darkness, "I'm out of here, tonight."

From the darkness came Tesco's voice, "I'm with you."

"You ain't leaving me behind," Kimo said.

They grabbed Osca and went to find Bullet. "You coming, Bullet?" they asked.

He nodded yes.

They all snuck out of the dorm, and once outside under the stars and moon, Kimo asked, "Where we going?"

"I got to see my grandma," Runaway said. "Sister Superior told me yesterday that my grandma couldn't come see me for Christmas. I'm going to see her, I know she's not doing well."

Tesco said, "You got something good to eat there, I'm hungry."

"We'll cook up a big Christmas meal," Runaway said.

They took off jogging and within an hour were miles from the home. They cut down an alley. Went over a lady's backyard wall. To keep their morale up, they sang low, rearranging, adding, or subtracting lyrics, and sometimes making them so funny they laughed.

They were afraid, but no one wanted to admit it. Thanks to their music, the excitement of the adventure was greater than their fear. They were alone, boys without parents, in a world suddenly lit up with Christmas lights and families enjoying the feeling of loved ones around the dinner table. It was disheartening to feel they were apart from the world in this way, but it was also invigorating to know they had each other.

Along the way they ducked into a yard and Kimo stole a hen. Osca and Tesco found eggs and nestled them into Osca's T-shirt. Bullet pulled off his sweatshirt, tied it into a makeshift sack, and filled it with apples and apricots he found under some trees. Runaway and Tesco ventured into Nolan's Meat Market and came out with a plastic quart of green roasted chilis, a pound of tamales, and a bag of cookies.

All around them as they traveled through the dark fields and along dirt roads, ditches, and paved roads, happy sounds of

Christmas mixed in with police sirens. On occasion, strangers arriving home yelled for them to get home to their families. Church bells rang. Nativity scenes glowed in windows. Trash cans beside houses brimmed with torn wrapping paper and shredded strands of colored ribbons, ripped-open department store boxes, old bicycles, and computer keyboards and monitors. Runaway salvaged a nice warm coat from a Dumpster for his grandma, and Kimo, not to be outdone by anyone, lifted a huge potted plant from the porch of a rich house and carried it on his shoulders. A woman at a red light saw them dash across the street carrying these things and, without taking her eyes off them, called someone on her cell phone.

One by one, the boys stole bicycles left unchained in yards until they all had one. Riding with one hand on the bars and the other clutching stolen goods, they yelped and hollered at each other joyfully.

After midnight, the streets and sidewalks were crowded with people going home from Mass, and as they sped through dark alleys, sirens and police helicopters became more numerous and got closer to them. They cut through a park and raced away from a pit bull snapping at their heels. Partying teenagers in cars screeched down blocks and around corners as house lights came on and residents stood in doorways drinking and laughing and stray dogs scuffled in alleys for trash-can scraps.

At dawn on Christmas morning, chilled to the bone, weary and famished, the five boys finally rode into Grandma's yard.

Runaway called out to her and opened the front door. He found her in the back on her bed. She looked frail and had lost a lot of weight, her gray hair had thinned, her eyes had purple rings under them, and she smelled sickly—Runaway saw that the flesh around her ankles and wrists was badly swollen and had turned a faint yellow color.

"Grandma, we came to see you, spend Christmas with you. Merry Christmas," he said. The good cheer in his voice was now replaced with barely concealed worry on his face.

"Merry Christmas, my sweet dove," his grandma said. Her voice ached with fatigue. She leaned heavily on him as Runaway helped her from the bed.

"Grandma, I brought you a coat for Christmas. I brought my best friends to see you too. We'll make you a good Christmas breakfast."

As Grandma wearily sat on the couch, trying her best to pretend she was feeling good, everyone pitched in to cook breakfast. They emptied whatever she had in her refrigerator and cupboards, and Runaway defrosted the green chilis, then peeled them and roasted them in the oven. Kimo plucked the hen, cut it up, and fried it in the pan, burning Osca in the process. Tesco was singing and dancing as he made a fruit platter and a pot of fresh coffee, and Bullet warmed and buttered a stack of tortillas.

After everyone ate, Runaway put the new coat on Grandma and they all went out behind the trailer, where Grandma sat in a big old wooden chair and the rest found stumps and bricks and bald tires to sit on. Kimo placed the big potted plant next to her.

She told them it was the best Christmas she had ever had, and they had made her happy. When she asked them where they were all from, Tesco and Osca shared how they wished they were back with their relatives in Jamaica. They told Grandma that when the civil war broke out in Jamaica, their parents were killed, and they were sent to live with their aunty in Oklahoma. When their aunty was arrested for using drugs, the authorities put them in an orphanage there that burned down, and then they were sent here, to the home in Albuquerque.

Kimo said he never met his dad, he lived with his mom in Utah, and growing up, because he was different, he got into a lot of fights with the white kids who made fun of him. One day, after the police took him to juvenile hall for the tenth time for fighting, they called his mother to pick him up but she never showed. He hadn't seen her since.

"Those are sad stories," Grandma said.

After a while, Runaway asked, "What's yours, Bullet?"

Bullet was hesitant at first. And then he started, "I lived with my grandma and grandpa, herding sheep in the prairie, and one evening these men came to our place and killed them both. They were drunk, on drugs, and crazy. They did things to me too, afterwards. I didn't remember a lot of what happened, until they brought me to the home."

They were silent, watching snow that had started to fall.

Grandma said, "Help me up, please." Runaway led her to the trailer door and followed her inside. She had Runaway pull an old suitcase out from under her bed and bring it to her. Sitting on the old couch, she set the suitcase on her lap and opened it.

"This is your Christmas gift, sweet dove."

Runaway saw the old photo album, some religious medals and crosses, and a big black Bible.

"I want you to take these things."

"But Grandma, these are your photographs . . ."

"I'm getting old, sweet dove, and my mind is fading. I forget things. I don't want to lose these things, so I want you to have them. And this," she said, taking out the Bible and opening it. The inside was hollowed out and stacks of money were perfectly bound and wrapped with red and blue rubber bands. "There's twenty years of my social security money. I'd say about sixty thousand dollars. I want you to have it."

"Grandma!" Runaway cried, "I'm sixteen, what am I going to do with that money? And why are you doing this? Grandma, why . . ."

Runaway started crying. She took his head and placed it against her chest and patted him.

"Shh, shhh, sweet dove, it's okay," she said. "I've listened to your dreams many years. With this money, make your dreams come true. You'll need this when you go. They're not taking you back to the home. Go live your dream, and with every penny, think of me, each penny is a love kiss from me to you."

"Where you going, Grandma? What's happening, Grandma?" Runaway hugged her and said, crying, "What's happening, Grandma, don't go away!"

"When you get to where your heart takes you, come back and see me, maybe I'll go with you and we'll live together," Grandma said, as if she had just thought of it. She followed up excitedly, "Yes, my sweet dove, send for me and we'll live together. That sounds like fun. I'd love that. Come on, let's go outside."

The boys had built a fire and grouped around it warmly. They stopped laughing and rapping when they saw how red Runaway's eyes were. Grandma had her kerchief out and she was wiping her nose and eyes.

"Oh, it's so wonderful when it snows on Christmas, isn't it boys," she said.

"What's in the suitcase," Bullet asked, suspicious that Runaway might be leaving him.

"Stuff . . ."

"Clothes and things?" Tesco asked.

"Other stuff." Runaway looked at Grandma, leaped up and hugged her, and broke down crying again. "Why you doing this, Grandma . . ." He cringed, and his face wrinkled up in the darkest sorrow the boys had ever seen. They'd never seen him that helpless, that vulnerable, and that hurt.

Without a word, Bullet rose and hugged his friend. He kept hugging him.

Grandma said, "You're going to be okay, sweet dove, you'll be fine. But you better go before they come. Ahh, this coat is nice and warm."

"Go where," Osca asked, alarmed.

Runaway turned from Bullet and looked at his grandma, wiping his eyes and face with his forearms but still sniffling. "Sure Grandma, okay, and I'll never waste a penny, I promise, I'll use it to make my life better."

"That would make me so happy, sweet dove, so happy, to know you've used the money for your dream, to make your life better."

The fire crackled and sparked and it started to snow harder.

Runaway hugged her one last time, mounted his bike, and told the rest, "I'm going to the bus station to get a ticket to California. Whoever wants to come, let's go."

They rode off into the snowy distance until they were completely obscure. The old woman started coughing, a terrible fit of choking and gasping, and when she spit, her saliva was red. She shivered and rose slowly from her chair, gradually toddled to the door, and went in.

A few hours later, when the cops came to pick up the boys, they knocked and knocked but no one answered.